Siege of Contraries

Rose Helen Mitchell

Siege of Contraries

This work is dedicated to Keith with my enduring love
and heartfelt appreciation for all our years together.

Siege of Contraries
ISBN 978 1 74027 602 3
Copyright © text Rose Helen Mitchell 2010

First published 2010
Reprinted 2010, 2011, 2012, 2015

GINNINDERRA PRESS
PO Box 3461 Port Adelaide SA 5015
www.ginninderrapress.com.au

Patrick

1

On an August night in 1917 I sat amongst a mixture of Irish, Scottish and Australian infantry units at a rest billet near the desecrated village of Fleury. The final battle for the city of Verdun had left it, and surrounding areas, in Allied hands. Now and again, an escapee from a swarm of flies feasting on a pile of horse dung nearby landed on the letter I was writing to Caitlin. A blob of blood lay splattered on the page. I drew a circle around it and wrote 'dead fly'.

'Got the flies daein' the censorin' eh, Paddy?' Jock Macpherson called out as he struggled with a canvas bucket full of water and a broken rope handle trailing along the ground at his feet.

'Well, Jock, I'm sure that between the blessed flies and the MO there'll be few enough kind words left on the page. Now, where would you be going with the bucket?'

'Ah've jist been doon at the river. The watter there's best for makin' tea. Why don't ye go on doon an' mix wi' the boys? It's jist fine for a wee dip.'

'Maybe later,' I answered.

The population of Fleury had fled from the destruction of 1916 and my unit was allotted an old lime-washed farmhouse that had a workable stove with a pile of logs stacked beside it. Miraculously, water still ran from taps in a room that could've once been a kitchen.

I heard footsteps thumping back and forth across the tiled floor. Metal crashing against metal. An out-of-tune voice singing 'Keep the Home Fires Burning'. I guessed it was Andy Muir. Andy had vowed to get the ancient black cast-iron stove that dominated the room working again. He'd stripped and cleaned the knobs, lids and doors from the monster and reconnected the flapping stove pipe to its base. The day before, he'd found useable pieces of Delft crockery hidden inside the stove. He'd carefully packed them ina straw-filled basket then hid the lot in a corner under a bedraggled blanket.

When I asked why, he'd said, 'In case the family get back – some o' them dae, y'ken.'

To bar all interruptions, he'd stuck a notice on the half-door entrance: 'Restoration site. DO NOT ENTER.'

Men had spent the morning unwinding clay-crusted webbing from around trouser legs and boots before pounding them in troughs of water. Sticks of charred trees behind our quarters made perfect drying hooks for long strips of puttee, socks and shirts. From where I sat, it looked like an army of scarecrows sending semaphore messages.

By the time I'd finished my letter and gone down to the river, the other men had gone, and so I had the pleasure of feeling I was the only being in the universe. I lay in the water and turned my eyes and ears far, far away from war and death to watch white puffs of clouds scudding around in a summer sky. No sight or sound of a soldier screaming in pain, nor even a single fly bothering my ears. For a moment or two, I could've been lying in the upper reaches of the Shannon.

Later that day, Watson, a barber from Aberdeen, had set up shop. His customers sat on a canvas-covered sugar tin and every now and then he'd bend and dip into an old leather bag. He'd pull out an assortment of scissors, razors and brushes. He gave no consideration to style. The only distinction between the dozen or so heads he trimmed was the colour of hair.

No one complained.

The talk around the barber's chair was all about Jenkins, and the soap he'd taken from a deserted house earlier that day.

Watson said, 'Trust Jenkins. People pinch precious things like paintings or crystal. He filches soap. Hey, Soapy, you smell so sweet, I could kiss you.'

Jenkins called out, 'Kiss my arse, you smarmy bastard!'

'Hey, Soapy, where's the rose , then?' Watson again.

'Sorry. Only lavender today, m'lud! You want roses? Have to go to Blighty for that!'

I left them to their horseplay and set off alone towards the Hotel de Ville. The path took me alongside barbed-wire entanglements that bordered craters holding the corpses of men who'd crawled in there to die. I changed direction towards the river and stopped near a solitary willow tree to consider the shape of the sky. I pulled out my journal and wrote (for Caitlin in my next letter), *Broken lumps of cloud whirling across a knife-coloured sky like wreckage on a river flood. Green leaves. Pale gold afternoon. Distant slashes of white that could be farm buildings. Sun spotlighting a solitary willow tree, the fronds trembling like girls caught in the arms of their young men.*

My mother's voice came from across the water, 'Now, son, on the days when the waste of war is everywhere, imagine a host of colours that I'll be sending you to bless your day.'

I focused then on the steeple of a Renaissance church rising above battered buildings on the road ahead of me. I'd been in that building and I remembered the smells of incense and candle wax that had tickled at my nose while mumbled, whispered prayers fell into my ears, wrapping me in familiar Latin rituals.

I reached the main square of the town, and was just about to enter the hotel when I was nearly flattened against a wall by a bronze titan wearing a slouch hat tilted over one ear, and a brilliant red poppy tucked behind the other.

'Sorry, mate,' he blustered, reaching out to steady me. 'Better get your skates on. Beer's arrived.'

'Well, now, that's a fine way to make friends.' I laughed, picked up my cap and dusted it off.

'I'm Harry,' he said. 'Who're you?' He offered his hand.

I took it. 'I'm Patrick and it'll be no good at all if we miss the festivities.'

'Too right, Paddy. Sounds like the party's started already.' Harry towered above me. He had the kind of face that looked like it was always ready to laugh. Lips tilted upwards and clear, sharp blue eyes beneath eyebrows that could've been fawn-coloured shrubs.

We quick-marched together into the noise and cigarette smoke. Lamps hadn't yet been lit and, at first, all I could see were shadows slouching, sitting or standing in groups against a dark wall. Then pale white faces emerged above bodies dressed in khaki. Some wore shorts above wrinkled socks and worn boots. Others had open jackets that showed braces attached to serge trousers tightened around the ankles with puttees.

The venue had once been a small country guest house. The interior walls had been demolished, making the whole ground floor into one large reception area. The floor was a patchwork of tiles, wood, and hard-packed earth. Black knotted wooden beams running the length and breadth of the ceiling lowered the roof so that men, the height of Harry and more, ran the risk of having their heads bashed. Broken spars and slats of wood climbing to the upper floor at the rear of the room looked like they had once been a clumsy and steep staircase. A rusty empty brazier sat in a hearth and beside that an ancient dresser chipped and scarred but still functional enough to support platters of breads and cheeses and bowls of fresh fruit. Windows, above a line of washing troughs on one side wall, were still intact and remarkably clean. An arrangement of tables and chairs assembled from bricks and boards were lined around the walls. The only decoration on the wall was a lone lopsided framed picture of the building dated 1912. It hung suspended from a silk cord, like a grace note of survival.

'What d'you do in the army, Paddy? Harry asked.

'Well, now, I spend time with the dead arranging burials, and when there's no bodies to bury, I find things for people. My official title is Procurements Officer.'

'Great! Let's procure a couple of decent chairs and a corner where we can watch the action.'

So we teamed up on a reconnaissance trip to the cellar, where we found a dozen mixed bottles of Beaujolais and Cabernet Sauvignon. And hiding under cobwebs as thick as skin, twice that number of the country's best cider.

We found a battered old couch with three legs, and lugged it up the stone cellar steps. Using broken bits of bricks for the missing leg, we settled into the best accommodation in the room.

Musicians with mouth organs, spoons, clappers, combs and paper began playing lively jigs and reels. Feet started tapping; graceless dancers galumphed around like two-year-olds in a parody of a military two-step. From a group in a far corner, I heard, 'It's a long waaay to Tipperary…it…sa long waaay to go-o-o.'

Harry's pal, Tom Paterson, formed a two-up school for Sassenachs and while we watched, Harry gave a fine commentary on the game.

'Y'see Patto over there? He's what we call the Boxer, and the bloke in the middle of the ring is a Ringie. The player who tosses the coins is the Spinner. Are you getting the gist of the game?'

'Well, I'm wondering if that bit of wood in the Spinner's hand has a name.'

Harry sniggered, 'Jeez, Paddy, your education's been sadly neglected. That's what's called a Kip.'

The gamblers circled around the two-up area and shouts of 'Foul toss' and 'Come in, spinner' punctuated moments of silence, like the kind you'd sit through at a benediction service. When the coins flashed in the air, the brouhaha started all over again.

Other soldiers sat around telling each other about close shaves with shells and how many Germans they'd killed and making exaggerated claims about how many women they'd had since they'd been in France.

A shipping clerk from Liverpool had one group hooting with laughter with his tale about a French liaison while on a two-day pass from camp. 'She was gorgeous: chestnut-coloured hair in a coil doon to her waist. Brown eyes you could swim in an' a figure like Aphrodite. Three months since I'd had a woman, I was desperate. Anyway, she invited me in to meet her mother and we had a loovely coop o' tea and fresh-made bread wi' jam. Next thing, I wake up in a fetid ditch wi' a scrawny dog lickin' at my face. Boots, socks, wallet and ring missin'. Can't trust these fooken frogs!'

By this time the men around him were doubled up laughing.

'Sorright for youse to laugh, but if ah go back to ma wife ringless, she'll 'ave me goots for garters!'

The men were now bathed in streams of gold from the setting sun sifting through the windows. Lines that had been carved on faces by the hardest of times softened in the glow. I watched as identities materialised and the burden of war disappeared into a fog of unreality.

From where I sat, I could see the front entrance of the church. It had a slated roof where birds wheeled and swooped. The steeple rose above two intact stained-glass windows on the front wall. Between the window that gave me this view and the ruined church, rows of white crosses grew from weedy, unkempt grass. I watched a British officer limp along and stop at each marker. He stooped low, searching for something. Every few steps he untangled two walking sticks that supported him.

'You Irish, Paddy?' Harry asked.

'I am indeed. Why d'you ask?'

'Well, you sound Irish. My ma would tell you the map of Ireland is stamped on your face, but here you are, fighting for the English king an' country.'

'Would you believe this now, Harry? My family left Ireland for a peaceful and prosperous life in England.'

Harry laughed. 'Trust the Irish to gettit arse up.'

I watched while the officer collapsed onto his knees. It seemed to me that he'd shrunk to half his size. I felt like an intruder into some sad story and moved away to join a singing group. 'Mademoiselle from Armentières' rang out loud enough to scare a family of doves away from their home in the rafters.

Drinking and socialising went on past midnight, when the men staggered back to their units in twos and threes. Hoarse voices sang slurred and off-key songs. Harry and I were the last to leave.

'Where you bayshd, Paddy?'

'Langley, Berkshire.'

'You shilly Irish bastard. I mean here in France! Where's your spot in the war?

'Well, now, my Australian friend, tonight, only God in his heaven knows the answer to that one.'

'Okay, Paddy, it looks like you need help to get home. Follow me.'

2

We lurched along for a few yards with our arms linked. Harry started singing a song he'd learnt while training in Egypt about sending Charlie Chaplin to the Dardanelles in his 'little baggy trousers and boots that needed blackening'. He turned his hat sideways, turned his feet outwards, picked up a stick from the grassy verge and twirled it around as he sang. His tottering movements matched the beat of the song.

Somehow we'd gone off the road onto a field. A clump of trees took shape in the moonlight and glinted on some kind of fruit. It looked like the branches were trimmed with silver balls. We wrestled with each other to reach the nearest branch first and it took no time at all to fill our pockets and hats with ripe red apples.

'Surely 'tis a blessin' from the gods now,' I whispered.

'Dunno why you're speakin' so low, Paddy, there's not another bugger aroun' to hear you.'

I trudged along behind him. 'Harry, 'tis a long road that has no turnin'. D'you think we could find a place to have a sit down?'

He pointed to a shape in the distance. 'There's a building of some sort.'

We picked up our pace.

'Harry, I'm wonderin' if maybe it's a house with a kitchen and people and home-made soup and music…'

'Christ, Paddy, your imagination's runnin' riot. A place to take the bloody weight off my feet would be good enough for me.'

A neglected ribbon of path bordered by thick grass about a foot high led to what looked like a barn. Three walls were intact and piles of straw made a grand retreat for two weary inebriates. The shelter was warm, dark and smelled of horses and rotting hay. It took less than a minute to poke the jagged ends of straw into submission and mould our bodies into the mound. Junk was strewn around but the edges of things were vague as if they lay in a penumbra of bigger things.

When my eyes adjusted to the light, I saw harnesses with dull brass fittings hanging from hooks. An old harrow, bent and rusting lay on its side. A dusty leather horse collar, cracked and worn, hung from wooden beams. Pieces of wooden crates scattered across the space made by the damaged wall had 'Pommes pour L'Angleterre' stencilled in black lettering.

We munched through a few apples until a scuffling sound startled me.

'What's up?' Harry asked.

'Wheesht. Did you hear that? Thought I heard something – maybe it's rats.'

The sound got louder and Harry bent his ear towards it. 'If that's rats, I'll eat my rifle,' he snapped.

We heard a groan. He signalled the direction. We crawled nearer.

'Strewth!' he shouted, pushing his hat to the back of his head as if the gesture would clarify what his eyes had registered.

A man lay amongst the straw.

Harry stood stock-still and looked around. Wary. Searching. 'Strewth!' he said again.

It was a sobering sight. We knelt down to get a closer look.

The man was young and blond. His brow was covered in sweat and there was a line of hardened blood from the side of his mouth to beneath his chin. Only his eyes seemed to move. The rest of him looked like a bundle of rags. We stared from one to the other and back again.

The man struggled, like he was trying to sit up. 'Korp…oral Karl Grot…ten…thaler,' he croaked.

Harry glared at the wounded man and stomped outside. 'Jesus bloody Christ!' he shouted to the night.

I heard him stride up and down, the tempo getting quicker, noisier, and each step accompanied by 'Bloody hell!', 'Goddamm bastards!' or 'Fuckin' Krauts!'

I felt bewildered at the meanness exploding from his heart. I waited.

He blazoned his anger at the world around him. His rant lasted about three or four minutes.

The mud and blood on Karl's uniform had jelled together and in the dim light it was difficult to distinguish one from the other. As I looked up and down his body, trying to see where he was injured, he put his hand inside his tunic and took out a small tin. He offered it to me. With the exertion, the tin fell onto his chest. I bent closer to pick it up and noticed frayed, thick grey fabric around a bloody mess.

Then I saw a shard of shrapnel sticking out from his stomach. I sat stunned. 'Holy mother of Jesus!' slipped from my mouth in a hoarse whisper. I knew that the field dressing in my tunic pocket would be useless for a wound that size – might even do him harm.

Harry's pacing and cursing stopped. I heard sounds of muffled sobbing seeping through the night and saw him crouch down with his head in his hands. I was pushing straw under Karl's head and around each side of him when Harry came back. I tore a rag off Karl's shirt and wiped the German's face.

Harry said nothing. He went outside again and returned with a dish of water. He dipped the cloth in the dish, cooled Karl's brow with one edge and moistened his lips with another. He took a closer look at the wound in Karl's belly, lit a cigarette and began pacing again.

'What's up, Harry?

'War's up – that's what's up. I'm tryin' to get my head aroun' what's here. We're trained to kill the Hun, Paddy. We never get to see their faces. I hate this bastard war!'

Again, I watched and waited.

'D'ye know, Paddy, back home when the Huns go about their day-to-day business, they get spat on, beaten up, lose their jobs. Shopkeepers won't serve the buggers. Three days ago I led a burial detail to retrieve what was left of fellas I'd fought beside. I saw Bomber Devine strugglin' wi' a body. Split in two it was. "Hang on, Bomber, lemme help," I said. Then I stopped and stared at what was left of me best mate, Danny Coffey. His legs were six feet away from the rest of his body. I used to go out wi' his sister. She died last year. She was seventeen – consumption. Danny was only nineteen, for Chrissake! I put his body together as best I could an' carried it to the burial detail. His mother and my ma are best friends. How am I supposed to nurse this bastard here as if I cared about him? Goddamn! God-bloody-damn! I wanna finish him off. I wanna finish off the whole fuckin' German army. Kill every bloody Kraut in France!' His lips clamped shut against each other.

From his tightly shut eyes I could see tiny pearls of tears slip from the corners while his Adam's apple worked overtime to swallow his anger, hatred and grief.

He went outside again. He paced the yard with arms spread wide and fists clenched, and all the time cursing. Then he stopped. Stood still.

I moved towards him. 'Hatred – 'tis a terrible thing, Harry. It turns your heart sour and leaves no space for love.'

His next words nearly choked him: 'Fair go, Paddy. Right now I don't need a fuckin' sermon.' His chin rested on his chest and his arms fell listless at his side.

It seemed to me that all the sorrow in the world was in Karl's albescent face and Harry's anger. The former drained of all colour, all energy, barely breathing and the latter spewing hatred from a tortured heart.

Two cigarettes later, Harry stretched out his hand to me, and then he offered the German water.

'*Gut… Danke schön*,' Karl whispered.

In an effort to transfer some heat into the shivering body, Harry and I sat each side of him.

After a moment or two, Karl pulled my hand towards the top pocket of his tunic and pointed to a wallet. Inside the wallet were some letters and a few photos.

I spied a rosary nestled in the curly, sweaty hair on his chest. I put my hand to my own chest, where a medal of St Christopher lay warm and comforting against my skin. My mother had put it around my neck the morning of my departure from England. I grasped the thought that the Pater Nosters and Ave Marias offered in Langley for the safe return of a son would be echoed in some German home.

Harry picked up the crucifix at the end of the rosary, looked at it and dropped it as if it was covered in slime from the battlefield. 'Didn't do you much good, mate,' he uttered, cocking his head to the side.

'You don't believe in the power of prayer, Harry?'

'Nope. I'd rather tell lies an' fornicate than pray to some idol for courage or salvation.'

Karl drew my attention to the little tin, now lying by his side. It was labelled 'Players Navy Cut Tobacco'. Inside were two pieces of paper. One was official and typewritten, the other a handwritten scrawl. I deciphered the words *auf Urlaub* and *Erlaubnis* and Karl's name and some dates. The handwritten paper was dated three days ago.

I showed the tin and papers to Harry. 'Would you look at this now, Harry. Where do you think he got it?'

'The thieving bastard probably pinched it off some dying Tommy.'

'But isn't that the way of war, Harry?' I showed him the papers. 'See here, it looks like our patient should be on leave right now.'

'Looks like he's going to be on leave permanently.'

'Y'know he's only a boy, Harry. Just like you an' me an' Danny Coffey.'

'I wish I hadn't seen his face…know his name.'

I held one photo close to Karl's face. 'Who?'

'*Mutter*,' Karl sighed.

A second photo showed Karl, gallant and groomed with a young blonde girl by his side, against a background of medieval buildings and cobbled streets. A mountain behind the buildings dominated the scene. Karl and the girl held skis upright in opposite hands. A white patch around their eyes showed where ski goggles had been. Each had a corsage of white flowers pinned to their jacket. They clung to each other, laughing.

When I held the photo up to Karl, fat wet tears the size of a sixpence gathered at the corners of his eyes, then slid slowly down his face through mud and blood to the edge of his jawbone.

Written on the back of the photo was 'Garmisch, Dezember 1916.'

'I've been there,' I said to Harry. 'Went with a group of student friends on a skiing holiday.

'Yeah? What's the country like around there?'

'Mountain footpaths. Pine forests. Dormant beech trees. Trying to stay upright in soft snow while tying ski bindings. I remember too that snow-ploughing downhill was a challenge to my uncoordinated limbs.'

Harry sniggered when I told him about the time I'd stopped suddenly with my legs each side of a bush while other amateurs glided past.

I looked at Karl's face and pictured him amongst the health spas and ski schools of Garmisch. Was he a ski instructor? Had our paths crossed on the slopes of the Zugspitze?

He pushed the photos and letters towards me. 'Inge, Freundin. Take them,' he rasped and sank back into his pain.

At some time during our vigil, Harry became fascinated with the bowl we'd used for water. Painted in blue enamel, it showed black letters of the alphabet around the edge. A dent at the spot where P, Q, R and S should have been was scrunched up as if it had been used for target practice. The hands of a clock rimmed the hollow in the middle. Roman numerals I to XII for the hours were surrounded by the numbers 1 to 10 and, around that, the months of the year. 'Made in Germany' was stamped clearly on the underside of the plate.

'Harry, how many bullet casings do you think this plate would've made?'

'Well, I'd say, 'cos it's here in my hot little hand, two or three more of our boys are still alive.'

'D'you s'pose the family that lived here's been wiped out?'

'Nah! My guess is they're refugees in Switzerland or somewhere. Soon as this war's over, they'll be back here, growin' apples and makin' cider. That's what I reckon.'

'Ah well, isn't that the way of things these days, but I'm wondering about the little French people who ate and learned from this dish.'

Karl dozed.

Harry studied the injured man's face for a long time before drifting off to sleep.

I fed Karl sips of water, cooled his face and kept watch for any changes.

A few minutes elapsed.

Harry began to thrash about and talk to someone only he could see.

'Harry, wake up, it's a dream you're in.'

He shook his head and rubbed the sleep from his eyes.

'D'you want to tell me about it now?'

'Jesus, Paddy! I saw my mother huggin' Karl, and givin' him flowers. White flowers. I wanted them to be yellow like wattle. She was tellin' 'im to come home safe. My ma was thin and dressed in a dark coat and button boots - she wore a felt hat with the brim turned away from her face — the way she was dressed the last time I saw her. Her head just reached the man's shoulders and she was lookin' up into his eyes. I tried tellin' her that I left Australia in a ship not a train and that she was saying cheerio to the wrong person. She ignored me, like she didn't recognise me. Bloody hell!'

Sweat beads spattered his brow. 'Geez, Paddy, right now, I'd give anything for a cool beer… My throat's like sandpaper.'

It took seconds to bring water to him and, between gulps and sips, Harry carried on about the dream, hardly taking time to get the words right.

'A train puffed and waited while guards directed military personnel to carriages fillin' up wi' identical copies of this bloke here. The woman now, I saw her lips move and heard her say, "You're home now, Harry." Funny thing, Paddy, the mother in the dream was speakin' in German but I heard it in English. What d'you make o' that?'

'Sure now, Harry, it's strange things that happen in dreams. But sometimes there's a grain of truth residing in them.'

Harry ran his fingers through his hair a few times, and stared at Karl as if the explanation of his dream lay with the German.

It was a long while before he turned to me muttering, 'I'd rather be twelve thousand miles from here on my motorbike chasin' rabbits through the bush.'

'Where you from, Harry?'

'Small town in north-east Victoria…Numurkah.'

'Odd name that.'

'Aboriginal. Means war-shield.'

'What's life like there?'

'Bloody beautiful. Cold in winter, hot in summer. A country of flat plains, beef cattle an' sheep. The main street of the town is lined with giant peppercorn trees an' the creek is bordered by eucalypts, mainly ghost gums. Me an' my ma live in Meiklejohn Street, two streets back from the town centre. My old man went on the wallaby when I was two, an' Mum's brought me up on 'er own. When I was a little tyke, she used to take in laundry and sewin' and she'd bake cakes and pastries for the rich folk in town. She's so full o' Scottish ingenuity an' the thrifty ways o' her heritage, my ma. She's managed to buy our house. Since I started work with the local newspaper, she gave up the bakin' an' laundry and now she only does sewin'.'

'Your mother's Scottish?'

'Too true. She came out to Australia as a lass of eighteen, nanny to the family of a wealthy grazier. The family went back to Scotland after two years. By that time, Ma had met my old man so she stayed. She's got an accent as broad as the back end o' a dray.'

'What did you mean, "went on the wallaby"?'

'He went off one day lookin' for work an' never came back.'

'Were you close to Danny Coffey's sister – the girl who died?'

'Ye sure ask a lot o' questions, Paddy. Well, Elizabeth – Lizzie to most people – was beautiful. An angel. Sometimes I'd come home from school or work an' she'd be helping' my ma with sewin' jobs. Ye know, Paddy, she was a laughin' happy girl one minute and six weeks from the day she got sick, she died. Lizzie used to pester Danny an' me to let her come wi' us down the creek fishin' or out bush rabbitin'. One Sunday when we were about fourteen an' she was twelve, she came down to Broken Creek wi' us. We rigged up a rope swing wi' a knot on the end and tied it to a branch of a gum tree. We swung back an' forth across the creek yelling eeh haaaaa! an' yahoooo!. Elizabeth wanted to try it. So Danny held the swing, I helped get her settled around the knot and off she went. Halfway across, she lost 'er grip an' fell flat on her back. The rope went limp. Too high for her to catch an' too far away for us to grab. Somehow we managed to drag 'er out. She wailed about her dress and "What'll my mother say?" an' all the time her hair and face covered in mud. She screamed at us, "My ma will kill me. I hate you two!" Danny scrounged around for kindlin' and we lit a fire but Lizzie wouldn't get close enough to the fire and tryin' to dry her clothes was hopeless. Now she smelt of wood smoke as well as drippin' wet. She accused us of tryin' to set her alight as well as drown 'er. One of our nosey neighbours, who'd seen our predicament, told Mrs Coffey, who came bargin' down the street like a bull in season. We never got to the creek for a while after that.'

3

Three men in a barn was the entire known world. From where we sat, we could see no signs of civilisation. Slivers of moonlight coming through gaps in the walls and occasional remote rumbles, like heavy furniture being moved in a room overhead, reminded me that other things and other places still existed.

'What about your family, Paddy?'

'Ah well, now, I live in a house full of women. Mother, two sisters and Caitlin. My mother is as Irish as wet grass. The greatest talker of a talking nation, she can argue, prate and prattle forever. Her mouth never shuts or runs dry. They send me parcels. Cakes, pastries, socks, hankies and underwear.'

'Is Caitlin the sheila waitin' for you back in Blighty?'

'Could be. She writes to me every week… Been thinking a lot about her. I didn't want to make any promises before going off to war, and that's the truth of it. But you never know what might happen between us when I get home, if I ever get home.'

'How come she lives in your house? She a relative?'

'No. You ever hear of the Quintinshill rail crash?'

'Hey, is that where a battalion of Royal Scots were…'

'That's the one.'

'Yeh, a Scottish fella told one of the blokes in my unit.'

'Well, Caitlin's parents were on that train. Her mother and mine were friends since schooldays in Ireland. Her only living relatives are a couple of bachelor uncles currently doing time in Killmainham jail for beating the b'Jesus out o' their rivals in the war for Irish independence. Caitlin's never met them, so it was arranged that she'd make her home with us.'

'Have you and she been walkin' out together?'

'Sure we have, now. The night before I left, she and I went up to the Bijou Theatre in London to see *The Pirates of Penzance*. We had a grand time. Usually, me and my friends team up with my sisters and their friends for weekly dances or parties but that particular night, everyone else was otherwise occupied. I believe there was much whispered conspiracy to get Caitlin and me out alone.'

'Sounds to me like in Civvy Street, you'd be posh, wouldn't say shit for a shillin'.'

'The word's "shite", Harry.'

We laughed.

Then we heard incoherent whimpers and snatches from Karl about '*Mutter*' and 'Inge'. At one point in his delirium, he sat up straight. His face glowed, his eyes fierce and bright. For a moment, when his pain seemed to have disappeared, he sang a halting verse that sounded like a folk song:

> *Frisch weht der Wind…*
> *Der heimat zu…*
> *Mein Irisch Kind…*
> *Wo weilest du?*
> *'Inge, es schneit dicke Flocken…schön.'*

'What's he sayin', Paddy?'

'Don't know for sure. Something about snow and Inge and somewhere beautiful.'

'Don't know where you are, mate. No bloody snow here,' Harry snorted.

The first light of a new day had just come over the horizon when Karl died. Harry found two pieces of wood and made a cross. He scratched 'Korporal Karl Grottenthaler' on the crossbar with a piece of charcoal. He tugged the dog tags from the dead man's chest. He took identification papers from an inside pocket and insignia from his uniform. Finally, He gently opened Karl's mouth and placed one of the tags under his tongue.

'Why you doing that? I asked.

'That's how the Germans do it,' he croaked.

I took the rosary from around his neck and the wallet and contents. We both wanted to keep the tobacco tin. I won the toss. We found a couple of rusty shovels, dug a shallow grave and buried him near the apple orchard. Harry placed his poppy on the grave and I recited the *De Profundis*.

Nothing more was said.

We were only two hung-over drunks with hay poking out of our boots, straw stuck in our hair and the odour of horse dung all around us on a summer night in a French apple orchard.

4

Today I'm in my room trying to say lines from Yeats's 'Presences'. The poem is on page twenty-four of a collection given to me by Caitlin. The flyleaf is inscribed, 'Welcome home, Patrick, from Caitlin. October 1918'.

I can see my old life within the romantic words of the poet. When I try to speak these lines, the rhythm and beauty of the poem is contorted. What I read is warped by the impediments in my speech and all sense of it is lost – more's the pity. The u sound is all right but the ahs and ees and ohs that I need have no distinction at all. 'From going-down of the sun I have dreamed/That women laughing, or timid or wild' sounds like 'Fmm gong dn uf w hun awhf drooomd aht nmn maufn au tivid oh imd'. Beguiling phrases that tripped off my tongue before the war now sound like the whine of an imbecile. My tongue, fused to my lower gum, refuses to budge around the syllabic sounds. Strangely, though, Caitlin is easy to say. It sounds almost normal. 'Caitlin…Caitlin…Caitlin,' I say again and again. I savour the normality and the tenderness that's in her name.

Lines like purple blood vessels spread up from my neck where my jawbone used to be. They meet in a carbuncular knot of mulberry-coloured flesh on my left cheek. It pulls my eye down so that it now sits near my left nostril and tilts my head permanently towards my left shoulder. Pale yellow blobs decorate my neck like some macabre theatrical image. Sometimes, when courage allows me to stand in front of the pier glass, I cover the disfigured side of my face with a piece of cardboard to remember how I used to look. Then I cover the good side and see only mutilation. The damage caused by mustard gas causes my breath to rasp and whistle, letting my family of women know I'm near, like a cat with a bell around its neck.

At mealtimes my sisters coax me to eat with them but, to tell the truth, I dread the smacking and gurgling sounds I make, and the awkward angles necessary to get food into my shrunken maw.

At dinner the other day, I tried to laugh with the others at Bridie's parody of her Red Cross supervisor giving orders to the volunteers. Something stuck in my throat. I couldn't breathe. I gagged and snorted. Water streamed from my eyes and nose as if a tap had been turned on somewhere inside my head.

Molly, my youngest sister, leapt up.

'Slap him on the back, Molly,' someone called out.

'Aisy now, Patrick… Breathe slowly through your nose.'

A tender, softer voice urged, 'Keep calm, Patrick. Keep your shoulders down.'

Just then, a glob of food and saliva splattered across a basket of bread and stained the white table linen. Bridie shook salt over the mess and Caitlin picked up the spoiled bread.

My mother coaxed, 'Aisy now, Pat. Sip slow now,' offering me a glass of warm water. ''Tis only a bit of a setback,' she said and four pairs of eyes watched me.

I felt their pity. Trembling like a dog in a wet sack I wheezed upstairs to my room. I moved slow enough to hear my mother say, 'I declare to God, gone from here these two years past an' all he has to show for it is pain an' disfigurement.'

A weight like water, rather than stone, pressed on my chest.

Sometimes I'm afraid to leave my room. It's now my entire world and the four walls of the house are my horizon. When I dare to look out to the garden and to the fields beyond, I visualise how they looked in the summer of 1916, when the leaves of the beech trees were luminous, and glorious summer colours edged lawns and laneways. Now, bare black branches and hedgerows drip with winter rain or take cover under snow.

Theatre programs and dance notices stuck on the mirror and cupboard door remind me of a secure, predictable life: weekdays spent in scholarship with friends of like minds, and weekends filled with the music and craic amongst family. My book-piled desk lies neglected and applications for next year's studies have been abandoned, like old socks in a corner. Letters from Oxford friends are stashed, unanswered, in a drawer and shadows lurk behind a screen that hides my future. I feel like a ship wrecked on a reef being flooded through a gouge in its hull and slowly sinking. Indeed, when I remember the mud-filled, rat-filled, flea-filled trenches in France, the thought forms a chasm to separate me from a society I once happily inhabited.

Christmas preparations are under way. I can tell plum pudding is in the making from the noises and smells coming up from the kitchen; the rattle of platters and bowls being assembled and counted; the clash of saucepans and the murmur of voices. Occasional words like 'pudding' and 'pork' are allowed to escape up to my room and I consider how easily abstractions move around the house while my body moves so slowly.

5

On a late September day in 1918, a bullet shot through the left side of my face taking flesh and bone with it. I remember. Shrapnel bursts. Bombardment. Artillery fire. Pain. Falling on my back. I remember clutching my face and feeling something ooze through my fingers. Then, a feeling like cold water coursing through my veins, making my whole body shiver. I'm thinking, 'If the warm liquid on my hands is my blood, why am I so cold?' I saw a flurry of yellowish cloud, and nothing else.

Later, I was jolted awake by the racket and vibrations of a field ambulance and a deep voice saying, 'It's all right, laddie. You'll survive.'

I saw a dark head and a Red Cross armband on his arm.

The randomness of it all amazes me. A place. A bullet. A puff of gas. An assignation with Lachesis, the apportioner of life, in a juncture of time, and my lifespan is determined.

Sometimes I think about that particular bullet. Who made it? Perhaps it had been forged by a young girl. Was her name Anna? Elsa? Perhaps she had sung *Deutschland Uber Alles* as she filled the cases containing the destiny of young men she'd never know. Perhaps she was preparing a comfortable home for a sweetheart fighting for Germany on the Western Front. Perhaps weapons made by her counterpart in another country ended his life in some bog-bordered battlefield in France, near where I was hit. I wonder, did this girl have lips soft and kissable and hair that shone in sunlight like those of the young girls I knew before the war? Did she ever learn that her industry ended the pleasure and sensation of romance for young men like me?

There is an unavoidable surety in all of this: her labour collaborated with the fates to forge the destiny of men from places as distant as Sydney and St Etienne.

6

The beginning: a warm summer night in August 1916. Anchored like limpets to each other by bulky kitbags, we could hardly move. The sound of a folk song accompanied by a mouth organ faded as the barque carrying over three thousand men moved off.

I lost sight of the red and green lights across the harbour. Above us, grey fat gulls swooped in circles then disappeared into the melded blackness of sky, sea and smoke belching from two giant funnels. Tiny bright sparks of light from cigarette ends darted around like fireflies in a giant jar. Engines chugged and throbbed. Grey-white faces smiled, glared, tightened lips and stared into the darkness. Some talk. A little song: 'Pack up yer troubles in yer ol' kit-bag an' smile, smile, smile.'

Scuffling feet sounded like sandpaper scraping on wood – impatient and urgent as if their owners couldn't wait to get to war. I managed to shuffle closer to the ship's railing and undid the top button on my tunic. The iodine smell of seaweed took over from the stink of cigarette smoke. I concentrated on the sound of lapping, slapping water against the side of the ship and the feel of a soft breeze playing with the fuzz on my cheeks and chin. I pulled my coat collar up around my ears. Farewells I'd tried to avoid still rang in my ears.

Molly: 'Don't forget to keep your feet dry, Pat.'

Caitlin: 'Watch out for those young French girls. Did you pack your journal?'

Ma: 'Be sure to stay warm now, son. 'Tis praying for ye I'll be – every blessed day. Have ye enough money now?'

Bridie: 'Write as often as you can, d'you hear?'

Ma: 'Will there be others travelling wi'ye, now?'

'No, Ma. To tell the God's truth, I'll be fightin' the war on my own. D'you think the Huns'll run scared? Don't you, any of you, be worrying now. I'll be home before you know it, so keep the kettle boilin' on the hob.'

'While you've a lucifer to light your fag, smile boys, that's the style…'

My mother had fastened a chain around my neck and tucked a little medallion into my shirt saying, 'Saint Christopher'll go aisy on ye, Pat… He'll bring ye home to us.'

'Sing us a song, Pat,' Molly said, patting me on the back.

Caitlin slipped her hand into mine. Then she led the way downstairs and out on to the street.

I took a deep breath and started,

> The minstrel bo-oy to the war is gone,
> In the ranks of de-eath you will find him.
> His father's swo-ord he has girded on
> And his wild harp slu-u-ung behind him…

I mock-marched to the corner of our street and turned around to see a tableau of four standing by the garden fence. Different heights, different ages, four arms raised and four white hankies waving in the wind. When I waved and walked out of their sight, I felt again for the note Caitlin had put into my top pocket. I still have it, and know every blessed word of it.

Dear Patrick

Parting from you leaves me with a heavy heart. I will miss the sight of you tramping up the hill on Friday evenings and the sound of your voice telling me about your week of exciting discoveries in scholarship. You will be sorely missed, and the songs we sing at the church socials will sound weak for the want of your fine tenor voice.

Patrick, my friendship with you is based on the comfort I get from feeling safe in your company. When I'm with you, I never have to weigh or measure my words because I know that you will sift the things I say, keep what is worth keeping, and with a breath of succour, blow the rest away. For that, I thank you from my heart.

I will let you know if I hear news from your Oxford friends, and I will keep you up to date with new literary publications. I will pray for your safety every day.

Patrick, wherever the road takes you, please know that you are loved. Please be vigilant as you move through France. Don't stay away too long and fare thee well.

Your friend,

Caitlin

PS: I love your face!

7

Memories of arrival in France: dull, hazy images of soldiers crowded around equipment piled higher than the tallest man amongst us and instructions barked like a machine gun spitting bullets. I saw a line of men, the top of their heads encased in gauze, each with a hand on the shoulder of the man in front – like a chain gang. They shuffled along, unsure of where their feet should go. A young woman with blonde hair and tired eyes linked her arm under one of the slower soldiers. He never saw the glory of her smile, a smile that reminded me of Caitlin on a summer day.

As we boarded a train, I heard words snatched from conversations: the Somme; mustard gas; blindness. I watched horrified. Somebody said 'Poor buggers' while we slunk into our seats in silence.

I wondered why in heaven's name I'd volunteered for this jaunt. How would I survive without my books and the stimulation of debates about the state of things in the world I'd left behind?

At the end of that day, we boarded a lorry that teetered and weaved along rutted roads. We scrambled off the transports at dawn, then marched for miles with full gear in lines of four abreast until we heard the first sounds of battle. We slogged along, with an early-morning mist circling our feet and obscuring rifts in roads of liquid mud. We squelched and swore.

A cockney voice yelled, 'What stupid bugger put these 'oles right where my feet wanna go?' and a chorus of 'It wasn't me, it was 'im' was heard above laughter.

I remember seeing a broken wall of some house with one whole window, glass intact, trimmed with lace curtains blowing softly in the breeze.

Sometimes we'd spy a family labouring in a farmyard gathering eggs or feeding pigs. They rarely looked up from their toil and seemed inured to the sight and sound of foreigners tramping the paddocks of their property. We'd hear the occasional barking of a dog or see a cow tethered to a hedgerow and I'd imagine the lives of the people who might live nearby; perhaps a family with children and pets and books and music. Perhaps there was a mother who baked bread and read fairy tales to young children. Did she cover their ears to blot out the noise made by regiments of soldiers a few miles away?

Once, later in the war, in a village tucked away among stubbled slopes of wheat fields, I watched an old man drive a furrow on the skyline. High ground and twilight hid the rest of the warring world.

On a pitch-black night, I think it was November 1916, Gerry Hood and I got lost in a maze of disused alleys and small dugouts across no-man's land. Enfilade fire swept back and forth along the length of our position, and above that racket we could hear the shells droning across the sky and exploding. We crept along like weasels in a hole. It was hard to tell if the reverberations we felt along the ground were the result of the barrage or from our blistered, shaking hands and knees.

The crashing, banging, screeching and roaring of weapons assaulted my ears and I wished the blessed noise would slow down to whimpers and sighs, like those I remembered from the last time I walked out with Caitlin.

I had to contrive some way of keeping my sanity and steer my mind away from the horrors, so I quoted lines from *Paradise Lost*. I was raving on about 'man's first disobedience' and 'justifying the ways of God to men' when a voice came through the darkness like a phantom.

'You can quit the poetry, Paddy. You're home now,' and I felt rough fingers place my hands around a mug of hot cocoa.

In the trenches, it was easy to forget that you were a weaver in a carpet factory or a baker of bread and some men, far from home, used the war to re-invent themselves. One sergeant, on trench leave, posed as a wealthy bachelor. He met a young girl at a village café, who fell for his seductive lines and married him. They were happy for two blissful days before his commanding officer visited her parents to report details about a wife and family back home in Belfast.

When I received mail from home, I'd check the handwriting, the weight and smell of the packages, trying to guess the contents before cutting the string and ripping the wrapping off. When aromas of jam and biscuits hit my senses, saliva would gush into my mouth. And at the taste of these things, I'd picture my mother picking the fruit from the plum tree at the side of our house. I'd imagine her crooning while she picked, 'I'll taaaake you home againnnn, Kathleen', and I'd see bright speckles of longing for her homeland gathering at the corners of her eyes.

When I opened packets of woolly socks and gloves, the smell of our front room, something like the scent of pressed thyme, embraced me. I'd see knitting needles and fingers flashing like tiny duelling swords. Funny how I could hear what they said but the sound of their voices evaded me.

8

On the last Sunday before I left for the war, Caitlin and I walked in the country. The others were at home preparing a special lunch to mark my departure and to celebrate Caitlin's eighteenth birthday. The hemline of a white linen skirt wafted around her ankles when she moved. Thick black hair spread across her back and fell to her waist over a white blouse. She wore white stockings and shoes with button-down straps and high heels that raised her brow to the level of my lips. A brilliant peacock feather sprouted from a straw-coloured hat she clutched in her hand. Her eyes were blue as the sky above us and she smelled of vanilla and strawberries.

The end of our street marked the beginning of fields and lanes edged by bushes thick with rosehips and brambles. About two miles along one of these byways we stopped at a farmhouse where Sunday walkers often bought chocolate and cool drinks. Caitlin and I sat on a bench in the sun sipping lemonade while a family of geese wandered around the cobblestone yard and an old border collie rested in the shade of an elm tree.

Strolling home, we spotted an orchard with apples ripe and ready for picking on the other side of a brick wall. We looked at each other. She nodded. I winked, leapt over the wall and thrashed my way up to the best of the fruit.

'That's enough, Patrick. I can't hold any more!' Caitlin called out as apples spilled over the edges of her hat.

We found a grassy spot and rested our backs against the trunk of a chestnut tree with a hat brimful of apples between us. We offered first bites to each other and licked the juicy sweetness from each other's chin. Colour was everywhere: azure, emerald, scarlet and the electric colours of a peacock feather.

'"Thou, sun, art half as happy as we…nothing else is."'
'Who said that?'

'I did.'

'No, Patrick, who said it first?'

'John Donne – 1572–1631 – writing to his wife, Ann More.'

'Will you write poems to me while you're away?'

'Ah well, now, Caitlin, that'll be a pleasure to me. Will you write to me?'

'I surely will. Will we still be friends when you come back from France?'

'I'll be your friend for as long as I live, Caitlin.'

She tickled my chin with a zephyr touch. 'Love that dimple, Patrick. D'you think you'll take up your studies when you get back?'

'That's a consideration for the future, Caitlin. Who knows what changes there'll be?'

She slid one arm behind my back, the other over my chest and rested her head against my shoulder. She whispered into my ear, 'Patrick, just come home.'

And the idyll ended with smiles and soft, warm kisses.

9

July 1917

Langley

Dear Patrick

I hope the socks fit. Your sisters and I used our own feet as models. We had great fun deciding on colours and patterns, and I hope you find the little notes we stuffed inside before you put them on. It wouldn't do for you to get blisters now, would it!

Remember the day we pinched apples? Apparently old Mr Wilson spotted us. He said that as you are not here to scale the wall and climb the tree this year, he will keep us supplied with fruit. He's just left a basket from the first harvest at the kitchen door.

Bridie and I are busy most evenings doing volunteer work for the Red Cross at the church hall. We make up packages of things that we think the soldiers will need. Let me know if you hear any comments from other men about the contents of parcels they receive. It would help us a lot in our work to know what things are most appreciated.

I'm not sure if you have read Joyce's Portrait but I am sure you won't mind reading it again. People here are excited about it. The enclosed copy is a gift for you from Michael O'Meara. He is desperate to hear your opinion of it. I think he is currying favour in the family – he and Molly have been walking out together. A future brother-in-law perhaps?

When time allows, I walk along the country lanes, full of our times together, recalling the smile on your face – like it was the last time I saw you.

More and more homes in the village have shuttered windows and mirrors draped in black. We heard that Frank Armstrong and Pete Easton, who were in the debating club with you, died at Ypres. We don't know details about when or how.

Patrick, I wish above all things that you will come home to us so that we can complete the half of our life that 'yet remains unsung'. Yes, Patrick, I am reading Milton. When you return, we can test each other.

We talk about you at every opportunity, Pat. Please look after yourself.

Much love to a beautiful person who is my friend.

Caitlin

***

September 1917
France

Dear Caitlin

Greetings from somewhere in France. I'm not allowed to say where exactly but I can tell you that the noise level surpasses the racket you and the others make in the kitchen when cooking and planning the next party.

At mail call today I got two parcels plus a bundle of letters from home. Six from you. Thank you. Thanks also for the socks. I surely needed them. You don't know how much it means to hear that you are well. You are a constant in this unstable life, Caitlin – the reality that keeps me sane in the midst of 'this hateful siege of contraries'. (If you find the source of that quote, I'll treat you to a posh dinner.)

Fancy Old Man Wilson delivering a basket of apples. Give him my regards.

Thank O'Meara for the book. Tell him he will, honestly, get a letter from me one of these precious days. He and I will have a lot to talk about when the war is over.

You'd be worried by the amount of waste that goes on here. It gets cold at night and sometimes kindling is scarce so field biscuits are sometimes used as fuel for boiling up dixies. It reminds me of the time when you and Bridie made a batch of scones for expected special visitors. The scones turned out so hard that we used them as coal for a week! Remember?

Yesterday, in a rare moment I watched the miracle of a clump of beech trees that had survived amongst blasted blackened ruins. I heard a lark. Its clear pure song was a perfect accompaniment to the movement in the trees and just for a moment I was reminded of Keats's 'viewless wings of poesy'. Silly bird, I thought. If I had wings I'd fly out of this place straight to your side and not look back. But it went on with its melody as if it were in heaven.

Yesterday when we were on the move, I felt hungry for home at the sight of candle lights flickering in a cottage window like glow worms in a cave. The image rescued me for one beautiful moment amongst the evil of carnage lying all around us.

As I write this, I am watching women and children huddled close for comfort on carts trundling along tracks we have just marched over. Their faces are almost obscured by mattresses and bundles of household goods. This same scene is repeated over and over again. It is almost as if it is the same people, amongst the same goods, on roads with no beginning and no end. I wonder, what terrible sins could they have committed that sentenced them to this seeming eternal displacement? The contrary side of all this, Caitlin, is now I'm seeing children, squeezed together on this pathetic chariot, laughing and playing pat-a-cake, slapping each other's hands, the way young people do in a school playground on a sunny day.

There is so much more I would like to say to you, Caitlin, but it can all wait for a better time. Give my love to the family.

Yours,

Patrick.

10

Christmas Eve 1917, France

Poppies had faded from the fields of France. Autumn rains and tramping armies had pulped them into something resembling clumps of overcooked spinach. Ice and snow spreading over the land froze ditches and potholes and sandbag fortifications and men's toes and fingers and ears. All, everywhere around, was black white and shades of grey.

An armistice had been announced to enable troops from both sides to bury their dead and my job was to receive bodies and arrange the order of burial.

I saw one cadaver frozen stiff, with its knees curled up to its chin and a fist stuck in its mouth, as if he'd muzzled himself to avoid crying out with pain and so attracting enemy fire to others near him. He was seventeen years old, the youngest corpse brought in that day. He was from a Welsh battalion and I thought about the wonderful songs from the valleys of Wales he'd no longer sing.

Many of the graves dug that day contained only a limb or, in some cases rags of uniforms with ribbons showing evidence of past conflicts. I gave thanks for the icy temperature that held the stink at bay.

Invisible seeds lay just below the surface of the battlefield waiting for April, when they'd spring green and red into life, nourished by the bodies of allies and enemies alike. Would the colours be more vivid next year than those of other years? Would the flowers reincarnate with the names of fallen young men engraved on the petals?

I heard quiet shuffling and a voice saying in a hushed reverent tone, 'The body…it fell tae bits. The ony way ah could rescue it wis bae shovel an' sandbag.'

I recognised the young private who'd been telling me earlier that day about his family life in Inverness. His arms and legs were jerking as if some agitated creature was attacking the nerve ends in his body.

'You look like you need a break, Ross,' I said, loosening his blackened frozen fingers from the sack.

He walked to the nearest empty space and vomited. 'Sorry 'bout that,' he croaked, 'but ah'll bide beside ye tae the joab is done.'

And so we worked as a two-man team until the corpses were lined up and tagged for internment. By sunset the job was done.

Men scrubbed the muck from their bodies and clothes the best way they knew how. Some wept, some swore, others were silent.

Johnny Carrol sat barefoot trying to loosen the mud caked onto his socks. He murmured to Jock Macpherson beside him, 'Y'know, Jock, the Germans out there are just as dead as our men an' the Catholics are just as dead as the Protestants.'

'Well, Johnny, the bard said, "Man's inhumanity to man makes countless thousands mourn." Ah dinnae think the lines apply to a partikler race or creed,' Jock replied, running his thumbnail down the seams of his kilt in the war against lice.

After dark, men sat around writing letters, playing card games and enjoying the peacefulness. No sounds of artillery were heard and no flares lit up the sky. It was a clear night with bright moonlight. I gave thanks for the fatigue that clouded my senses and allowed a blanket of exhaustion to lull me away from war towards scenes of Christmas at home.

I wondered what my women folk were doing. Were they at Midnight Mass? Were puddings swathed in calico sitting on a bench waiting for the big feast tomorrow? Was the front room decorated with paperchains? And were little parcels wrapped and waiting by the hearth?

I heard a vague sound coming from the German side. At first I couldn't quite work out what it was and strained my ears to catch it through the softness of the night.

Someone was singing. I sat up and listened. The Germans were singing Christmas carols!

Stille Nacht, Heil'ge nacht
Alles schlaft, einsam wacht
Nur das traute hoch heilege Paar
Holder Knab' im lockigten Haar
Schlafe in himmlischer Ruh!

I had sung this song in German many times during my school years. I'd never thought in those days that I would ever lie in a ditch somewhere in France on Christmas Eve, listening to a choir of young German men singing the same lyrics. I climbed to the top of the redoubt and spread my arms wide. I looked up to a sky full of unfettered stars and joined in the chorus. At first, the others looked at me, shrugged their shoulders and went on with what they were doing. Then slowly, one by one, they started singing. By the third verse, the voices of both sides blended over no-man's land and 'Silent Night' continued in tune but in English and in German.

I'd heard about the first Christmas of the war when fraternisation between Allied troops and Germans had been severely dealt with and when I spied a lone, brave figure moving through the darkness from the German camp I waved my arms and gestured with my hands as if to push him back. The moon was behind him and I could see that he wasn't wearing a helmet or carrying a weapon. A white flag on a stick waved gently above his head. The hymn still rang out from both sides, embracing him in a benediction. Soapy Jenkins broke from our group and started moving towards the stranger until they stood a few feet apart. The German boy stretched out his hand and offered a packet of cigarettes to Jenkins. Soapy accepted it and offered a handshake. When the song ended, Soapy and the German returned to their respective corners.

Before the night was over, Soapy was ordered to report to his commanding officer. We never saw him again.

11

Christmas 1918, Langley

The house is full of secret plans for the festive season. The kitchen is always warm and today it smells of roast beef, rosemary and cinnamon. The quantities of pastries and puddings being prepared would feed all the expatriate forces now wandering around London waiting for transport to their homeland. Someone is cooking apples and the aroma floating up the stairs triggers a memory of an August evening in 1917.

During a hiatus in the war, I sat outside a whitewashed building that could've been a cow byre or a pigsty. I thought that if I'd had the power of an artist I'd paint the groups sitting around me. Each in their own corner, perhaps whispering with knitted brows about some military grievance or agreeing with mutual smiles on some naughty nicety.

I heard Wollongong Willie shout, 'Anyone for a stoush?' He waved a cricket bat above his head.

Henderson answered, 'You got a ball?'

'Nope…well, kinda…need your help…follow me…be back in a jiffy,' he said in one breath, pointing Henderson to the side of the outhouse.

They returned a few minutes later carrying a bushel basket of apples. Two teams were organised: English infantry versus a mixed bag of Australian and French soldiers.

'Too right, Paddy, no game for weak hearts,' Watson said when I opted out. 'Just you sit there wi' yer books. But y'know, mebbe you'd learn more if you watched the experts.'

The contest ebbed and flowed around roars and bellows of 'Howzat!', 'You're stumped…get outta here!', 'It's a six!'

In khaki shorts and bare feet, they looked like ragamuffins at play but any onlooker would've thought they were playing for the Ashes the way they scrambled and shouted all over the place like a mad woman's breakfast. By the time the game was finished, the basket was empty. Laughter from two teams of larrikins, and the scent of splattered apples beneath their feet, sweetened the air around us.

12

When I enter any room these days, conversation is quickly forced behind pursed lips. So I sit on the edge of my bed for hours on end. Here at least I don't have to contend with their puzzlement and thwarted attempts to decipher my speech. Now and again, I drag my ancient satchel from the bottom of the cupboard. I stroke it and fiddle with the oxidised clasp then return it to its hiding place.

The mud of France, creased into the old worn leather, still clings to it like a parasite on a pig's back. Each time I look at it, I feel part of my soul is bound to the bloodied soil of Europe and I crawl mole-like into a mental burrow made black and grey with murky shades of men I'd helped to bury. Their shadows zigzag over the reality of home. Now, the bag sits open at my feet and for the past hour I've been unwrapping and re-wrapping souvenirs of a particular night.

Bridie rapped on my door, breezed in and pranced across to the window. 'I keep telling ye, Pat, ye need to let God's good light in… It's not good for the soul to sit constantly in the dark! Didn't you say you'd keep the blind up? Didn't you, now?' For the second time that morning, she raised the blind, making the room light with winter sunshine.

I shrugged and turned my head away.

'What you doin'?' she asked, plopping down on the bed beside me.

I pointed to the notice on my door that I'd stuck there years ago. It had yellowed and curled over time but the quote from Juvenal still applied: 'Here; it is women who may not cross the threshold: None but males can approach this altar.'

'Oh, indeed now! We don't take notice of that when you want something now, do we?'

I find myself resenting my sisters. They are so full of stupid important things like fashions and food and dancing. They think they are doling out comfort but they are denying me my solitude.

My sadness is that I no longer fit into the life of all the things I have longed for, prayed for, fought for, and waited for. My old life has stayed where I'd left it and, for me, the dividing line is too wide to breach.

Bridie looked at me in her engaging way, signalling an interrogation.

I reached for my notepad. I wrote, *I'm trying to decide what to do with these things.*

Bridie picked up the packet labelled Karl G. 'Who's he?'

Somebody I knew for a little while.

'A German?' she whispered.

I nodded 'Yes.'

She looked at the balaclava lying on the floor. Every letter I'd received still snuggled inside it.

'Where did this one come from? It wasn't made by one of us.'

It's a gift from a young soldier from Manchester.

'Did he survive?'

Don't know. Never saw him again after the night he gave it to me.

'Do you want to talk about the war, Pat?'

No. Not yet, not to you.

I pulled out my journal and showed her the entry for a particular night.

15th August 1917

Harry disappeared.

After a few minutes he returned carrying a cardboard box. He moved slowly and handled the package with care. He put the box down in the middle of the floor.

'What ye got there, Harry?' Paterson called out, 'one o' your mother's lamingtons?'

'You're about to find out Patto. Right, boys. Gather! Let's have some fun wi' frogs.' He moved around like an auctioneer inciting a group of bargain hunters. One arm held high, one finger pointing to the ceiling, calling out rules. Then he made a wide circle around the box with old window cords he'd found lying around. 'OK, fellas. In this box I've got some of the finest frogs you'll find this side of the equator. Numbers 1 to 12 are painted on their backs. Choose your number and place your bets – whatever you consider worth winning. No money. Paddy over there'll collect whatever you've got to offer. When I lift the lid and the frogs start jumpin', first one over the line wins, for the owner, everything in the kitty. And they get to keep the frog.'

There was uproar, the likes of which could be heard in an English pub on a Saturday after football. Someone offered a hand-knitted, full-face balaclava. Soapy Jenkins managed another cake of soap.

'You said you'd used your last one, you sneaky bastard,' Murdoch whined.

Cigarettes, socks, biscuits, shell casings (some engraved with initials and dates) and tobacco tins (some with tobacco) piled up in front of me. The table became so stacked with goods; keeping the contributions in some kind of order was like trying to straighten the edge of the Irish Sea.

Frog number one was the favourite.

Harry strutted around the outside of the circle waiting until the hubbub died down and all attention was focused on the box. He stepped into the middle of the circle. 'Are you ready, frogs?' he asked the box.

Wise guys from the crowd answered with 'Ribit, ribit, ribit.' Harry lifted the box. The race was on. The crouching frogs looked like newcomers to some town, faced with a six-branch crossroads. Throats pumping, eyes bulging, splayed feet stuck to the floor. For two or three minutes nothing happened. The men became silent. Then one frog hopped, then another, and another.

All hell broke loose. Men shouted.

'Move, ya fat four-legged bastard!'

'Keep it up, number two!'

'Show us yer stuff, number six!'

Tin mugs rattled on terracotta tiles making a racket like an amateur brass band at their inaugural practice. Men, faces clumped into the colour of a radish skin and shouting to their chosen frog, hopped around the floor, like children at play.

'Hop like this, ya fat turd!'

'Jump like this, moron!'

'Whip 'em up, Hughie!'

Two frogs seemed to make it over the line at the same time and Harry called on me to settle the dispute.

In the end, a young private from Manchester collected. He gave me the balaclava as compensation for my good judgement. 'Can't stand woolly hats,' he said, staggering away with tins of jam, cigarettes, matches, socks, a cricket bat, a load of Machonochie's tinned rations, and Soapy's last(?) cake of soap.

The event became known as The Great Race of the Frogs.

The rattle of the front door knocker interrupted us. Bridie tossed my journal onto my bed and leapt to her feet. She jumped the stairs two at a time to attend to the visitor. I'd never seen her move so fast. A few minutes later I could hear bumping and scuffling of feet on the staircase and loud whispers outside my door.

Caitlin, the lambent light from her eyes spearing into me, announced, 'Hey, Patrick, we were saving this surprise for you for Christmas Day but it's arrived early. Close your eyes.'

All giggles and nudging, they crowded by the half-closed door. I pushed the satchel and its treasures to one side, put my hands behind my head, sprawled on the bed and waited.

'This what you do all day, ya lazy bastard?' Harry, still in uniform, stomped through the doorway with four chortling women behind him. I could see that his fourteen stone of taut, trained muscle was still intact.

He agreed to stay for Christmas and for the next few days his voice, booming against the walls and furnishings, blasted the house out of a state of near mourning. On one of these mornings he showed my sisters and Caitlin the finer points of making shortbread biscuits and damper. I watched from the doorway.

'You must sift the flour three times then draw it into the butter like this,' Harry lectured, exaggerating the actions of a pastry cook. While they cut stars and angels from the dough, they sang Christmas songs.

I liked Harry. I liked the way he drove people on during this time. In the evenings he helped to make garlands from strips of coloured paper cut from magazines. He and the girls draped them around the walls of the front room. Watching the fun from a chair in a corner, I felt invisible. I looked and listened to the chatter around me and it seemed to me that Time had pushed my sisters back to a younger life while it had pulled me forward into old age.

13

On Christmas Day, Ma in her usual place at the table started the festivities. 'We'll have a toast now, so will ye all fill up your glasses.'

Carafes of sherry, ginger wine and cider were handed across and along the table.

'Let us salute these two darlin' boys sittin' here with us on this blessed day after fightin' to preserve this life of ours. Well done, boys. Oh, and welcome to our humble home, Harry.'

Amid the chink of glasses, Harry looked along to me and winked as if to say, 'You did tell me she was a talker.'

The centrepiece of the table was a giant platter holding a goose glowing amber and garnished with translucent orange circles. Plates of pork and ham, tureens full of golden roasted potatoes and greens shone amongst cruets of gravy and sauces. Wine glasses, water glasses and silverware were like commas in a paragraph of a yuletide essay.

'Harry, mebbe you'll do the carving honours,' Ma asked.

'My pleasure,' he answered picking up the nearby tools.

Before we started passing plates and food around, Bridie moved to the Victrola in the corner, cranked it up and the feast began to the voice of John McCormack singing 'Keep the Home Fires Burning'.

When he'd finished slicing into the meat, Harry stood up. 'An' here's a toast to you and to yours, Mrs O'Hare. This is the best time I've had in years. Thank you all.'

'You're heartily welcome, so you are,' Ma beamed at him.

In spite of my mangled mouth, I managed a few morsels of pork and half a glass of sherry but mainly I sat back and watched and listened to the banter that lasted until the serving dishes held only remnants of food – a bone here, a bit of crackling there.

Molly cleared some space and fetched the fattest ball of plum pudding I'd ever seen. 'Knowing this is your favourite, Pat, we doubled the ingredients this year,' she said, putting it right in front of me. 'Would you do the honours now?' She handed me a bottle of brandy.

Somehow, I managed to stop my hands from shaking while pouring the spirits and setting the pudding alight. Blue and yellow tongues and spires of flames waved, settled around their target and faded out like spectres in a bright light. Everyone clapped and ooohed and aaahd at the sight and smell of it.

Molly found a little gold key in her portion. Somehow it had separated from its paper wrapping. She giggled and sucked at the pudding residue on it.

'Watch now, Molly, you don't want to swallow it,' Ma said, 'else you'll never be able to give the key of your heart to Michael O'Meara.'

Molly blushed, wrapped the key in her hankie before hiding it in a corner of her dress pocket. Caitlin pouted when I got the ring but she perked up and smiled with eyes big and wide when I wrapped it in crepe paper and gave it to her.

'It looks like I'm to be left languishiing on the shelf,' Bridie moaned when she found the thimble.

Harry found a silver threepenny bit. 'Now I'll never be short of a bit 'o silver,' he said, sticking it in his shirt pocket. 'I'll keep it forever.'

My mother lapsed into what I called her Irish state. Her eyes glazed over and she started to sing and talk in Irish. 'Now you'll soon be leaving us, Harry, I understand… *Nil aon tintean mar do thintean fein.*'

Harry looked across at me scratching his head.

'It's Irish for "there's no place like home",' Caitlin piped up.

'An' I tell ye this, m'boys, ane o' these God-given days, I'm goin' home to the oul' sod, but right now I'm thirstin' for a cup of good strong tay.'

Harry jumped to his feet and gave her the tightest hug. 'Show me where the tea caddy is,' he said, and moved towards the kitchen.

Molly thumped out tunes on the old piano and as the others sang 'It's a Long Way to Tipperary', Ma weaved around the furniture carrying a shillelagh like a banner.

Harry joined in singing the old songs of farewell and reunion.

While they sang till their voices were hoarse, lumpen knots of melodies shook in my throat, jammed tight as if under a rusty lid on an ancient container.

'You're all singing like linties,' Ma said.

'What's a linty?' Harry asked

She laughed. 'Och now, the English would call it a linnet, but whatever label it wears, it's still the sweetest sounding bird you'll ever hear. Now, Harry, how about you give us an Australian song?'

'Me sing? Ye ever heard a pig chewin' a brick? That's the noise you'd hear.'

'Now, listen to me, Harry. Everyone can sing – it's not like you're competin' for some kind o' trophy…'

'I tell ye, I wouldn't know how to start. But I can go better'n a song. I'll tell you about Christmas in Australia.' With that, he moved to the hearth and stood with his back to the fire. He hooked his thumbs in his braces and began:

> It chanced outback at the Christmas time,
> When the wheat was ripe and tall,
> A stranger rode to the farmer's gate,
> A sturdy man, and small…

And for twenty-three verses, he paced out the pattern of 'Santa Claus in the Bush'. He turned this way and that way, he imitated the 'dour gude wife' with a long face and skinny eyes. When it came to the bit about picking up the emu's egg, he bent double, and you'd have thought he was carrying a newborn infant in his empty arms the way he rose to his full height and took slow careful steps to where Ma sat enthralled. She played the game and accepted his armful of air. His laconic drawl and precise actions hypnotised us, so that when he'd finished we sat stunned for a long minute before clapping and cheering his performance. Harry bowed and grinned.

Caitlin fetched him a glass of water. When he sat down she asked, 'What's Christmas like in Australia, Harry?'

'Well, for one thing, the climate's a lot different. Hot as hell. It's a struggle to keep food from spoilin'.'

'How does your mother manage, then?'

'We've a good cellar for storing food – built from stone a foot thick. Then in the kitchen we have a meat safe for things like butter an' milk.'

'D'you mean a safe like they have in the banks?'

Harry guffawed. 'Nope, it's like a wooden box on stilts wi' a front door. Hinges on one side, door latch on the other. Look, get me a bit o' paper and pencil an' I'll draw it for you.'

I handed him my notepad and pencil.

So for the next while, Harry muttered and scribbled, now and again ripping a page off the writing pad, screwing it up and tossing it into the fire.

Finally, he showed us his masterpiece. The specifications of a Coolgardie safe, cross-sectioned and drawn to scale.

Bridie asked, 'Harry, what d'ye normally eat for Christmas lunch in Australia? I mean, you wouldn't get much meat in that wee box.'

'Well, y'see, my ma thinks she's still living in the cold wastes of Scotland. She cooks an' bakes till she's in a sweat. Steak pie the size of a young pig is her specialty. Like you, she grows all our vegies. She does all the cooking real early in the mornin' before the sun gets too hot. We fill the house wi' neighbours and a fair number of folk that are sufferin' hard times.'

Half-eaten mince pies, and screwed-up paper hats lay abandoned here and there on the table amongst the red and green of holly twigs. Glasses rimed with egg nog adorned the piano.

'Would ye leave it all till later now,' Ma said when Bridie started to tidy up. 'Sure the wee folk might look kindly on us while we have a wee rest… I'm off to lie down now.'

The four women sidled off and Harry and I settled ourselves each side of a roaring fire, fixed in the chairs as if we'd been poured there in a liquid state.

We'd been sitting like that for an hour or so when my mother re-appeared.

She handed both of us a glass of whisky. 'I'm off to chapel now, to give thanks that you're both sittin' here by my hearth.'

She puffed and panted as she pulled on her galoshes at the front door, and I tipped my whisky into Harry's glass. Between cigarettes, Harry sipped at his drink. We both stared into the flames.

'Have you heard the one about the rabbits?' he asked

I shrugged 'No'.

'Well,' said Harry, 'there's this old couple, Jock an' Jean, who've been married for about a hundred years. They make a pact with each other. The deal was that whichever o' the pair died first, they were to come back from the other side an' let the survivor know what it was like. Well anyway, Jock went first an', sure enough, one night when Jean was getting ready for bed, he comes back. He says, "Jean you have to come here, it's great! We have sex before breakfast, after breakfast, middle o' the mornin', before lunch, after lunch. All day an' all night, its sex, sex, sex." "Oh!" says Jean, "all that sex in heaven Jock, I'm surprised." "No, Jean,' says Jock, "I'm no' in heaven, I'm a rabbit in Australia."

Our laughter bounced off the walls.

14

The next afternoon, Harry persuaded me to go for a short walk to the local tavern. It was bitter cold and threatening to snow. A trilby hat, a warm scarf and coat collar did their best to hide my face. The tiny hairs inside my nose froze, my eye lashes stuck together and my breathing sounded like a blacksmith's bellows.

Flames from an open fire were a welcoming sight and we sat on an old oak bench as near as we could get to the warmth.

Conversation between us was a game of charades. Besides me scribbling away, we parodied questions and answers by waving hands, closing fists, pointing fingers, raising eyebrows, nodding 'Yes' or gesturing 'No'. Crouching, leaning, and walking with peculiar gaits. Shrugging shoulders and spreading hands mimed acceptance or ignorance. Harry's antics had other patrons rocking with laughter. I laughed till tears ran down my wasted face.

One of the things I liked about Harry was his ability to take his own share of the good feelings he spread. And I liked the way he pretended to study the pub décor while I struggled to slurp at my beer, ignoring the dribbles slipping from the side of my mouth down my chin.

Do you remember the night we met, Harry? You had a poppy in your ear.

I showed him the note. Harry's expression changed. He looked past me like he'd gone off to some foreign place. I waited.

'Poppy,' he said quietly. 'It reminds me of a wilted flower on a makeshift grave.' His hands shook as he lifted his drink to his lips.

15

I hadn't been alone with Caitlin since I got back and when we returned from the pub, she and my sisters were in the kitchen discussing a dance to be held in the local church hall the next night. She was standing by the stove stirring and watching something in a pot. Her long, shift-style dress had a dropped waistline and her hair, now cut in a fashionable bob, gleamed clean. She looked up at me. Her eyes scanned my face. Questioning. I bolted for my room.

Harry found me pacing the floor. 'What's up with you, Paddy? She's a knockout!'

I scrawled, *Can't bear her to see me like this.*

'Well, Paddy, if you don't want her, let me know. I wouldn't mind a girl like that.'

The laughter of the past few hours evaporated. I paced back and forth across the floor, from the window to the wall, to the door and back again, many times. I felt the horrors of war grasp me around the throat and snap shut around me like a vice. I squirmed and hopped around trying to shake off the thousands of tiny barbed spikes attacking me. I held my hands over my one good ear to block out the noise of enfilade fire and closed my eyes against the sights of sandbags lined up against newly dug graves. I didn't see my friend reaching out or hear what he said.

All I saw were visions of burnt earth, trampled fields of flowers, and seared trees as if Envy had walked across the land.

I don't know how long the attack lasted. I only know that when I woke up from a deep sleep someone had covered me with a patchwork quilt. For a little while I watched the light from a lamp on the bedside table reflecting the colours of the spectrum into a glass of water beside it.

Caitlin sat by the window with an open book in her lap. I studied her face through half-open eyes. Unblemished before the war it now looked like it had been lightly written on with words like lonely and longing. Her red-rimmed eyes seemed to be counting the raindrops that splattered against the window panes.

'Caitlin.'

Her book fell to the floor. She turned to look at me then moved quickly across the room and switched off the lamp.

She knelt by my bed and, with a touch like a feather, caressed my brow and whispered, 'I still love your face, Patrick.'

We held each other tight and cried together in the dark for a long, long time.

When dawn was breaking I searched through my bag for letters I'd written to her while in hospital but never posted and handed them to her. I lay still and quiet watching her face while she looked through them and turned to face me.

'Now, Pat, the question is, what can we save of us? What's survived of the truth and loyalty of our friendship?'

My effort to find the right words came to a blessed halt when my mother appeared with a tray of breakfast food. She placed the tray on a small table by the window and looked me straight in the eye.

'Now, son, listen to me. I'm sick with sorrow for your plight, but tears and lamentations serve no good purpose. Look around at the richness of your world now and make the most of what you find there. Think about that now, d'ye hear?' She slammed the door on her way out, leaving her words to circle and sizzle inside my head.

The next day, Harry left for Southampton and the ship that would take him safely across oceans to the port of Melbourne; to big skies and acres of space. 'I'll send you some sunshine to brighten up this bloody country' was his parting shot.

For an instant, when he shook my hand I thought he was going to hug me. Watching from my bedroom window as my mother and sisters carried his bags to the charabanc, it was like seeing an impressionist's painting of a farewell on a rainy day. The collar of Harry's army greatcoat was turned up to his ears and his hat was tilted to one side. He bundled himself into the vehicle and never looked up. I could barely make out his face through the rain-splashed glass. My formal salute went unnoticed.

Caitlin

16

December 1918

A week before Patrick's return, a boy cyclist delivered a telegram. 'I like this one,' he said to Bridie. 'No black border.'

'Telegram!' Bridie called out, and three pairs of feet charged to the front door.

Kate ripped the missive open, collapsed on the nearest chair and wept. She handed the slip of paper to Molly. 'Read it, Molly. Hurry up, will you.'

Molly stared me straight in the eyes. 'It says, HOME SAFE. STOP. PATRICK.'

Kate's laughter sounded like the chiming of a church bell at a wedding. Bridie, Molly and me danced a jig in the kitchen, then collapsed breathless around the table to plan his homecoming.

Endless days. Watching. Every footfall and clip-clop had us jumping to the door. In the end, a heavy snowfall blanketing any sound from the street, and the darkness of an early winter morning, allowed Patrick to arrive almost unnoticed.

Earlier that day I'd put fresh linen on his bed, cleaned the windows and mirrors and polished the wooden surfaces with lavender polish. I'd hung bunches of rosemary in the window recess and replaced his books and papers on his work table the way he'd left them. I'd been busy tidying his suits and shirts in the wardrobe when I heard the slam of the front door closing and something bumping along the hallway. A voice saying something like 'Hu awh' brought me tripping down the stairs two at a time. I didn't recognise the figure who'd created the

noise and who now stood in front of me. I stood stuck to the spot. He
had a thick woollen scarf hiding most of his face and his head seemed
to be anchored to his shoulder. Then I saw his eyes.

Kate heard me yell out, 'Patrick's home! He's home!' She bustled
along the hallway and threw herself at him. She looked up to his face.
'Well now, at last, here's a sight for sore eyes.' She shouted, 'Holy
mother o' Jesus!' and clapped both hands to her face.

Patrick stepped back from her. He stood stock-still for a long
moment, well back from me. He spurned breakfast with us, struggled
upstairs to his room and locked the door.

During the next few days, the house took on a look of mourning.
We moved around quiet and secretive like, each with our own thoughts.
At mealtimes his mother or one of his sisters would take food up to
Pat. The trays came back almost untouched.

Deliverance from this despondency came in the form of a tall,
blond, hairy Australian. Within minutes of Harry Kenihan's arrival,
Patrick appeared downstairs for the second time since he'd come
home. He attempted speaking with Harry but his words coiled into
a mass and stuck in knots of purplish flesh. In spite of this, it felt
wonderful to see him amongst us again.

Harry could've been Irish the way he talked endlessly, marching
through one meaningful topic after another. While he helped us
prepare our Christmas Day feast, he told us how he and Pat had met
in the war. During the days of Harry's visit, brightness flowed around
me. I saw him as a stout-hearted Homeric figure whose life seemed to
be one long adventure of discovery. I liked the way he brought Patrick
out of his melancholy. It gave us hope for the future.

The day after Harry left, Patrick signalled that he wanted me to
come up to his room. He stood me in front of a long mirror on the
wardrobe door, himself beside me. He reached out and took my hand
so that we faced our reflections. We stood that way for a minute or
more.

Then he turned to look at me, 'Shee shis,' he wheezed, cupping my
face in his hands and holding it still. 'Oafn oor aise, Caitlin.'

The contorted sounds made my ears hurt. I felt my knees tremble.

Pat reached for a jotter. He'd written, *I want you to see what I've become.*

Can you bear to see this face every day of your life? He threw the book to the floor and grabbed me by the shoulders.

I lowered my eyes. 'Pat, please…please, don't… You're more than a face to me.'

The meagre scaffolding around his spirit crumbled like a balloon stuck with a needle and he flopped onto his bed.

One evening, I found him standing outside with his back to the sunset, his shoulders stooped. A balaclava covered his head and face. Only his tired eyes showed. I took his hand. He let me snuggle up close to him until the sun's rays melted into a soft gloaming. And so, by degrees, he admitted me into his space. He allowed me to hold him close when the tremors attacked him. He let me help unravel his stammers and stutters and we learned to deal with his fits and fears together.

A memory of a long-ago Sunday walk stirred and shifted to the front of my brain as if someone had pushed a button to start the machine of my mind. It opened up like a rose at midday, a new, hopeful omen newer than that very moment.

Instead of long conversations, we wrote notes to each other – news about veteran homecomings or items like the first flight from England to Australia. Our future lay in a penumbra of trivialities as if it didn't bear looking at.

Then, on a day in early spring, Patrick asked me to marry him. *Dear, dear Caitlin, 'let us possess our world in this little room. Not out of fear but out of love.' Will you?*

17

June 1919

On a bright June weekday morning in 1919, before the first Mass of the day, six of us stood in front of the altar through the ritual of Nuptial Mass – the short version.

The air and the gardens were full of new birth and scented by promises. The smells of incense and warm wax blended with the scent of roses and lavender. Molly and Bridie wore dove-grey silk dresses and cloche hats trimmed with a pink rose fresh from the garden to match the posy they'd made for me in the early hours of that day. Tiny drops of dew still lingered between petals as if they too were hiding their tears. Kate, in her Sunday-best bottle-green crêpe de Chine suit, hid her concern for Pat behind smiles of forced gaiety. Michael O'Meara acted as best man and, with Father Teehan, he did a grand job of keeping Patrick on his feet.

Patrick tried hard to say his vows but when it got to the part 'with all my worldly goods…' he resorted to writing. He did manage a firm, loud 'I do.'

Kate had organised two reliable women from the parish to serve our wedding breakfast and as soon as that was over, Michael announced, 'D'you see that cab waiting at the door? It's taking Molly, Bridie and Ma to the boat for Belfast.'

And so they went off to Ireland for a week, leaving Pat and me alone.

On the first evening of our honeymoon, when our supper had been cleared and the dishes returned to their usual place, I was sitting on a settle by the living room window. Patrick moved to my side. He tried to speak. But all I heard were grunts and snorts. If the sounds had been a colour they'd be black, or shades of purplish grey.

He took up his notebook and showed me what he'd been trying to say: *There are no words big enough to tell you how much I love you.*

I reached out and cupped his face in my hands and his big soft hands enveloped me. He pulled me close to his chest. He brushed my hair with his puckered lips and stroked my back. We sat, squeezed tight together like conjoined twins until he stood up slowly, pulling me to my feet. We edged upstairs, one step at a time.

Next morning while Pat was still asleep, I wandered around the garden. A grin stretched across my face until it nearly split in two and my body felt like every sinew and muscle and bone in it had been replaced by a just-born reproduction.

I washed fruit and cut bread for breakfast in a room full of radiance, as if the sun had coaxed the colours from the garden through the window to embrace me in a cape of brightness and hope. I could hear Patrick's breathing through the open doors and it seemed to me then that the panting, gasping inhalations and expirations I'd become accustomed to had diminished to the level of a loud, comforting snore – the kind you hear from someone sleeping on their back with their mouth open. I felt like I'd woken up from a horrific dream and been gifted with a new reality. Somehow everything around me took on a denser solidity; the dresser and the dishes on it glistened like they'd been painted in a soft light. For a little while, I sank into this wondrous new existence. It was enough.

18

December 1919

The way I remember it, I see Patrick and me sitting on a bench huddled together against a light breeze blowing from the east. A watery sun makes the temperature unseasonably mild but the air is still cool enough for hats, gloves and warm jackets. Window boxes on the sills along the front of the house are bare of blossoms and their spring coat of green paint is now mottled with faded and flaking patches.

Patrick, searching through his notebook, found a page dated a few days earlier. He showed me: *I never knew my father and would like to know that our baby will have someone to teach him (or her) the things a father should. When I die, I want you to marry again.*

I laid my hand softly on his arm. 'I don't want to talk about a life without you, Pat.'

He scribbled, *But you must, Caitlin… I'll die a happier man if you do and that's the truth of it.*

I watched his hand race across the page and felt big tears gather at the corners of my eyes. I turned my head away from him.

He unbuttoned his jacket, leaned his head low over my distended stomach and whispered something that sounded like 'Cgha ooo ear mne nnnow.' Then he started to hum a soft Irish lullaby.

I stared at the holly tree, dripping with red berries at the side of the house and stroked my fingers through what was left of his black curls. A wave of something like dread mixed with longing swept over me like a cold wind. I shivered. He raised his head and crushed my hands in his, then looked at me with the saddest, bluest eyes. I wanted to plumb the depth of them and drag out his pain the way a dentist would pull out an infected tooth.

He spread his fingers as wide as he could over my belly. At that instant our baby kicked. Just for a second Patrick's face took on a look I hadn't seen in a long, long while. Excitement? Elation? Rapture? He gagged. Almost choked.

When he calmed down, he scrawled with a shaking hand, *Would you believe that, now? I think the babby just did a somersault.*

'He's jumping for joy because you're feeling better.'

And what makes you so sure it's a he?

'Well, now, you just have to trust me on that one. I have a feeling. Besides, your mother and sisters did the wedding ring test over my bump and apparently that never lies.'

He started scribbling while I described how Molly, Bridie and I had taken my wedding ring off and slipped a length of thread through it. Then we suspended it over my belly. 'It's a girl, it's a girl,' Bridie whispered through excited giggles.

'No, look, it's changing direction.' That was Molly.

Bridie again, 'Try it again, Molly, and this time keep your hand steady.'

'So, Patrick, the final trial showed that our baby is definitely a boy. Have you thought about a name? I think we should call him Patrick. What do you think of that?'

Ah well, now…not Patrick. Me, my father and his father before him, have all had that name. That's the way of Irish traditions but I think it's worn out by now — time for a variation. If it is a boy, I have a fancy to name him Patricksoniel after Ireland's great liberator.

'But suppose the test is wrong and it turns out to be a girl after all?'

Mary Kathleen — doesn't that look grand on paper?

He was about to add something else when Bridie rapped on the window behind us, holding up a teapot and waving her other hand as if she was scooping air into the room. I helped Pat to his feet and we moved towards the warmth of the kitchen.

Sometime during that night Patrick developed a chest infection. He shivered so violently that the shadows on the wall shook with menace. By Christmas Eve morning, we understood that he was dying.

His room became a white-walled, firelit, silent place scented by the smell of candle wax. A small wooden stand by the bedside, covered with a shining white tabbinet cloth, held two candlesticks. Each held a long fat candle with wax drips dragging down from a black wick. A leather-bound Missal lay open at the *Confiteor* with a rosary sprawled on top like scattered jet beads.

Sounds. His stertorous breathing. An occasional sigh from his mother. The hiss and spit of sparks from a log in the grate. And the click-click of rosary beads slipping through fingers.

During the long vigil, Kate with her greying hair peeping out from a white mob cap and ties hanging straight and loose on her shoulders, hardly left his side.

Father Teehan arrived and stood by the bedside. His erect stance and precise intonations gave him more the appearance of a military man than a clergyman. He droned over points on Patrick's body, '*In nomine Patris et Filii, et Spiritus Sancti,*' while making the sign of the cross, with an oil-soaked thumb, on the sole of each foot, the palm of each hand and in the centre of his forehead. The sacrament finished, he lifted his embroidered satin stole over his head, folded it, closed his prayer book. Staring out the window as if he couldn't wait to get out of there, he gave the ritual blessing, '*Beannacht libh* (bless you). *Dominus vobiscum* (the Lord be with you). There's nothing more to be done here.' He left, closing the bedroom door with a quiet click.

I rushed after him and caught him in the hallway as he was putting on his over-boots. I wanted him to say he'd misjudged Pat's condition… that he'd been a bit hasty with the Last Rites…that Pat would recover. I wanted him to leave us with some words of comfort. The priest said nothing. He didn't look at me but scurried off to a waiting cab.

Outside, red berries on the holly tree made a splash of colour in a black and white world. Snow lay banked up against the picket fence. The bench we'd sat on a few days ago was now covered in crystals. A blue-black sky above me looked like a blanket pinpricked with a million tiny lights.

Molly joined me near the door to listen for the clop-clop of the horse bringing the doctor's carriage. She wept silently. Her arms, folded tight across her body, held back her grief. She tugged on my sleeve.

'Caitlin,' she whispered, 'I'm so sorry for your troubles… Michael says we'll postpone our engagement. We don't feel like…'

'You'll do no such thing, Molly. I won't hear of it. And neither will Pat, so don't be worrying a thing about it. We'll talk it all through at a more suitable time. Let me know when the doctor arrives.' I made my way back upstairs.

The ancient hinges on the bedroom door squeaked like a banshee and two pairs of eyes looked to the door startled.

'Molly'll stay downstairs for now,. How's the fire holding up?'

'It's okay for now,' Bridie said.

Kate faced Patrick's back. Her face, smooth and unlined, looked healthier than her son's. She began to hum a soft Irish melody while trailing her fingers with long, slow strokes along Patrick's spine. I sat mesmerised by the spot of blessed oil shining on his brow.

Now and again, Kate wet her fingers in a dish of holy water and let droplets fall on Patrick's form. Light from a lamp on the wall beside the door and a fire in the grate flickered and played tricks with our shapes - softening features into youth and health. It touched the gold band on Patrick's left hand ring finger and danced across the gloss of a framed picture of the Sacred Heart on the wall above his bed. I looked up to that image and remembered a time when Patrick had turned the picture to the wall before kissing me. Nobody else was home that day to hear the squeaks from the bed springs and our giggles that turned into sighs. And later, the moans of our passion in a rare moment of loving. How long ago was that? Months? Years?

The clock in the parlour chimed three when Patrick sighed his last breath. It was such a soft breath we hardly heard it. His mother bent low, put her cheek close to his mouth, looked at me and gave two slow, sad nods with her head. I tightened my grip on his still warm hand over my belly and just sat there, staring. Numb. Puzzled. After a long while, I took the pillow from under his head and pulled off the pillow case – squeezing it against my face and sucking in the smell of him.

Bridie scuttled away. She pounded down the stairs and up again with Molly in tow. They stood wringing hands and wailing sobs before reaching their arms out to me in a tight, tight hug.

Kate O'Hare stood up. She tilted her head, pushed her shoulders back and drew herself up to her full five feet height then bent and whispered close to Pat's ear, 'You've done your days in purgatory now, son. Safe journey to your place in heaven. 'Tis true enough, now, you'll never see grey hair, small blessing as that is.' She took two copper pennies from her apron pocket and placed one over each of Pat's eyes.

While I straightened his body, she stooped down and took the bed pan from under the bed and left me alone with him. I looked at his shrunken form lost in bundles of feather quilt and pillows and turned his head so that only the unblemished side would show. The absence of the gasping, rasping sounds from his chest and throat left me stunned. I wanted them back. I wanted to hear some living sign from him.

At times I heard the sound of muffled conversations, like the humming of bees, coming from the kitchen. Resonance. Movement. Pauses. And as I looked at Patrick, my thoughts sliced through the sounds the way a fish slices through water. A memory stirred and shifted to the front of my mind back to a time when he and I thought we were spring – the source of new life. I caught the smell of lemons mixed with other fruit. Apples? I heard the murmur of bees. I saw us sitting on a farmyard bench. Geese. A dog lying in the sun. Where was that? When was that?

When I'd washed his body and dressed it in the suit he'd worn at our wedding, men from the local church carried him downstairs and laid him out on a trestle table in the parlour. Candles were lit around him and a vigil was kept by him for a whole day and night before Requiem Mass and burial in the cemetery behind the church.

20

After the men had taken Pat, I lay for a long while half-awake on the white counterpane on his bed. I tried to bring back his form lying beside me. I picked at indiscriminate red and green flowers cross-stitched in the fabric and twitched my feet and legs. I lay on while the wind blew a billow of lace away from the window and the hem of it swept across the polished wooden floor.

The empty chairs in the bedroom looked like sentries standing to attention and the little table beside the bed held the forlorn, still-open Missal, rosary and holy water font. I wanted to break them into smithereens – smash every solid structure in the room – rend the curtains to shreds and tear down the walls with my bare hands. Ooooh, the pain! The tearing, bashing, battering pain in my heart! His suffering. His beauty so mutilated!

Through my agony I heard a dog bark somewhere. Muted sounds of footsteps in the snow seemed to reach my ears in a slow march.

When news of his death filtered outside, people came to the house from every corner of the parish. Some families, still grieving the loss of someone they loved, brought food – enough to cover every inch of the dining room table and spill over to a credenza on the far wall. The smell of steak and kidney pies, brown-topped crusty loaves, trays of buttered filled sandwiches and porter cake full of fruit and dark beer mixed with the scent of burning candle wax. People knelt and prayed for a few minutes then tiptoed to the kitchen where other folk gathered for the wake.

I wanted them, all of them, to go away.

On the day of Pat's funeral, the air was leaden and still. The headstones, the gates and the church came through a grey damp morning as if they'd been waiting with stretched talons to grab at my beloved. I tried not to remember the day when we'd walked, arms linked and proud in sunshine, through this same place with shiny gold bands on our fingers and crates of hope for Pat's recovery.

Harry

21

The train taking me back to Numurkah moved too slowly. From a corner seat I watched the landscape move along. I breathed it in and felt it race through my veins. Flocks of sheep, sulphur-crested cockatoos, cattle at rest and dark brown earth edging straw-coloured paddocks. Summer heat lay over fields swishing past. I wanted to stand on the carriage roof and shout my good feelin' to the world. Not a gun or a drop of rain in sight. I felt dazzled by the expanse of it all.

Other returning servicemen had left the train at Wandong and Broadford. I couldn't wipe the grin off my face when they waved goodbye and I was able to enjoy the scenery in solitude. As the train chugged onto the next stage, I put my feet up on the opposite bench an' shouted, 'Thanks, Hughie' for my good fortune.

The climb through the lower ridges of the Great Dividing Range ended at Seymour, where I wandered with other passengers to the station café. A cool beer and a meat pie slaked my thirst and filled my belly. I sat under a gum tree in the yard enjoying the feast and felt the sun seep through my shoulders, along my spine and into my bones, like a warm smooth whisky burnin' through every gland an' causin' me nerve ends to tingle. I felt the narrow drab skies of England leach out of me an' the mud of Flanders slide from my body. I imagined this must be how a snake feels when shedding its old skin. Magpies called to one another. A dog barked. I heard children playing nearby. It felt so good when strangers, seeing my uniform, waved 'Hello' and shouted 'G'day.' I wanted to hug them an' attach myself to the essence of them. I wanted to roll myself in the earth, to smell it and feel it on my bare feet. I took up a handful of soil from the pub garden, held it to my nose an' let it sift slowly through my fingers.

In my pocket book, where most men kept photos of their wives or girl friends, I'd put two dried eucalyptus leaves; the remains of those my mother had sent in her letters. They were from the river red gum that dominated our yard; the tree that I'd climbed as a boy to survey the world beyond our house. During the war, I'd stuck the leaves in my hat band, in my boots, inside my shirt. I'd often stuck them up my nose to help me cope with the stench of rotting flesh.

'What's that snot-green stuff hangin' from your nose, Harry?' a Cockney fella had asked me once.

'You ever seen a warralanga white gum? Or a river red gum, or a ghost gum shining on a full-moon night?'

'Nope!'

'Well, too bad for you, mate. You don't know what you're missin'.'

Paterson told me once that I looked like a bloody flower garden when he saw me with a poppy tucked behind an ear and eucalyptus leaves around my hat.

When the train passed the outskirts of Seymour, I spotted a game of football. It reminded me of a soccer game I'd watched with some repatriation mates in London. In the pub after the game, comments from our lot about the English national sport had nearly caused a brawl with the local lads.

'Call that football?'

'Nah, it's more like a bunch of fairies mincing along.'

'With a net that size, you'd think they'd at least make a decent score!'

'Come to Australia an' we'll show you a man's game of football.'

The publican happened to be an ex-rugby player. He didn't have to ask the blokes twice to 'leave peacefully or else'.

The countryside from Shepparton flattened out to brown pasture land before changing to acres of fruit trees that fringed the track on both sides. Peaches, pears, apricots, an' nectarines glowed ready for harvesting and saliva ran down my chin at the sight of them.

22

My home town was the second to last stop on the line. For the hour that it took from Shepparton I stood ready by the carriage door, kitbag at my feet, an' sweatin' hands ready to grab it for a quick exit. It didn't matter that I hadn't written to tell my mother the exact date of my arrival. In her last letter she'd told me,

> There's only one train a week to Numurkah and since the war veterans started to come home, the townspeople make a social occasion of each arrival in the hope that someone's son, brother or husband will be on it. So whenever you arrive, you'll be sure to get a welcome. I watch and wait for every train.

As the train lurched around the last long curve on the line across Broken Creek, I heard the beat of a Sousa march an' when I stepped from the carriage, you'd 'ave thought I was the King of England the way the people cheered and clapped and shouted.

'Good to see you, Harry!'

'Well done, boyo!'

A collection of mothers, farmers, councillors, bakers an' schoolchildren with their teachers crowded the platform. My hat got lost amongst the back slapping and kissing and hugging. Brightly coloured flags decorating the platform waved and a white banner across the footbridge blared, 'Welcome Home.'

My mother was at the back of the crowd an' the old kitbag came in handy as a batterin' ram to get me through the welcoming committee to her side.

When I picked her up, it was like lifting a ten-year-old child; I'd forgotten how tiny she was. I spun her around till we were dizzy. We laughed like loons, staggered for a minute then stood silent, grinning like conquerors.

'Hello, son.'

'Hello, Ma.'

I picked up my kitbag and started moving homewards. 'Let's go home, Ma.'

'Ye have tae dae the parade, Harry. It'll no' take long and they look forward tae it.'

Horse buggies decorated with streamers lined both sides of the road from the station to Melville Street. It had become part of the homecoming celebrations for veterans to lead a parade along this avenue to the town centre for an official welcome.

I looked around at the people who'd given me such a heart-warming welcome. 'I s'pose another hour or so won't matter but there's somebody I need to see. Gimme a minute.' From the corner of my eye, I'd spotted a well-known face. I left my mother in charge of my kit and moved across to where she stood. 'Hello, Mrs Coffey.'

'Hello, Harry. Welcome home.'

I gathered her in my arms and let her tears pour onto my tunic. People looked away and rummaged in pockets an' handbags for hankies.

As I looked past the station to the miles and miles of space beyond the western boundary of the town, I felt that I was on the threshold of a journey rather than at the end of one.

Nothing much had changed in Numurkah. Some businesses had installed the wondrous telephone and some houses, including ours, had acquired electricity. The streets were still wide and the river still curved westward at the end of Meiklejohn an' McDonald streets. Peppercorn trees still lined Melville Street. The great gums on the riverside still had knotted rope swings dangling from stout branches, now half-hidden by summer growth.

Everywhere I went in the first few days I carried a twig of eucalyptus leaves. Now and then I'd break a leaf in two and draw the fragrance through my nostrils; I couldn't get enough of it. It was strange and wonderful to feel the force of the sun on ordinary things like door handles, the cat's dish and outdoor seats. I looked at the height and breadth of the sky until the heat overpowered me. I wandered through each room of our house, touching the walls and inhaling the softness of home by pressing my face into curtains and cushions. I stroked the plants in the garden and broke sprigs from lavender and rosemary bushes.

Early each morning when a light mist lay on top of the water, I'd spend some time sitting by the creek remembering the times me an' Danny Coffey had ventured across raging rivers and built forts to repulse barbarians. I imagined that the war cries and laughter we'd shared back then were still around and if I stretched out an arm, I could pluck them from the air.

23

The week before I'd left for the war, I'd cleaned and polished every tiny part of my motorbike until each one looked like new. I'd draped it in scraps of soft material snaffled from my mother's rag bag and covered the lot with wheat bags. It'd sat like that during the years of my absence. When I uncovered it on that first night of my homecoming, an army of mice scuttled from nests inside the casings. When I remembered the rats that had lived in the trenches, these little pests were almost endearing. I checked all the corners and crevices for other rodents, gave the bike a quick dust down, then sat and admired it for as long as it took my mother to cook dinner.

The wonderful smell of home cookin' was second only to the taste of it. Lamb roasted in the old black stove and vegetables planted, nurtured an' picked by my mother, tasted like somethin' out of heaven. The bread pudding was pure ambrosia. The sounds an' smells comin' from Ma's kitchen reminded me of the time I'd spent with my Irish friend an' his family.

'This is a change from field biscuits and tinned bully beef, Ma.'

'Well, I hope there will be nae mair field biscuits for ye, and I hope that there'll be nae mair war. A' these young men…it's criminal… Bill Jackson came back a month ago. His brother got killed at the Somme. Ye know that bunch o' young larrikins that used tae hang aroun' the Globe Hotel?'

'Sure.'

'Well, four died in France and two have come hame wi' nae legs. The two McKinstry boys came hame in ane piece – a blessin' for their mother. They've now got jobs in Coxon's foundry. Dan Sullivan's got his old job back with Farrall the builder. I hope ye've purged the wanderlust frae your system, Harry, 'cos Klon Morris says ye can have your job back at the *Leader*.'

'Who's Klon Morris?'

'He's the boss at the paper now. There's been a' kinds of changes. It's got a new name - *Numurkah Leader*. I wrote all about it to ye last year.'

'Didn't get that one.'

'Do ye remember Kathleen O'Connor?'

'Sure. She was Lizzie's best friend.'

'She's my new helper. She's been askin' for ye. Would ye like me to invite her round for a meal sometime?'

'Not yet, Ma. I'll let you know.'

Most of my time in the first week was spent workin' on my motorbike. By the end of that time, the tin casings, engine, fuel lines, and nuts an' bolts were spread across the width of the shed. I cleaned and polished each piece includin' the spokes on the wheels until they shone like shafts of light. Now an' again I'd stop to listen to the sounds of home. A horse cloppin' along and a voice calling 'Rabbito! Rabbito!' followed by the sounds of housewives bartering for a bargain, reminded me of the times when Danny an' I had made enough money from dead rabbits to buy second-hand pushbikes.

When I heard the sound of the train whistle as it prepared to stop, I'd join the crowd headin' up to the station to greet the latest veterans. Always, when I heard the sound of children coming from school, I'd put my work aside, go to the front fence and watch them go past.

Then I'd remember times when Danny and I had snuck into Sunday school purely for the cream buns we'd get at the end of the session, an' how we helped Mrs Scott put tables an' chairs away so we could scam second helpings. Sometimes we'd wait outside until we heard the scrape of boots an' chairs on the wooden floors an' the clatter of tables being stored. Then we'd run breathless into the school room an' tell her a trumped-up story about charitable works keepin' us late for the lesson.

The sound I liked most to hear was the whirr of the belt an' the thump of the foot pedal on my mother's sewing machine. It was the most comforting, secure sound of home. When I was little, I used to stand by her side as she pedalled an' turned the wheel. I would hold the end of the fabric, fascinated, as it fed its way through the metal foot an' ended up stitched into a skirt or jacket. I liked it best when she was making curtains because then I stood well back and allowed myself to be pulled along with the material as it moved through to the other end. The word 'Singer' emblazoned in gold lettering across the black body of the machine was the first word I learned to recognise.

'Does the machine sing, Ma?' I'd asked.

'No, Harry, that's the name o' the maker, but we can sing while we work.'

And so at these times I learned the old Scottish folk songs my mother had learned as a child in Scotland.

24

The flatness of the bush country around the town had always fascinated me. The endlessness promised exciting adventures. Many times, when I was a toddler, neighbours had brought me home from my wanderings.

'Found Harry halfway out of town, missus – thought he was too far from home' or 'Found your boy on his way down to the river, and thought you might be worried.'

When I was about nine years old, my mother had helped me make a billy-cart. That first set of wheels took me further than I had ever been before. I spent my days trundling around searching for odd jobs and selling eggs from the chooks we bred. Sometimes Danny Coffey and I caught and skinned rabbits that ended up in the cookin' pots of poor families. Other times we'd have stone jars of home-made lemonade or jam, sometimes scones and cakes that my mother had baked. 'What have you got today, boys?' people asked, as they poked around our cart. It was a great feeling to be able to take home the pennies we'd earned.

The war didn't intrude into my daily life, but it attacked me frequently in the night.

I struggled to shake off the chains that tied me to battles like the one at Verdun that had lasted for six months. Sometimes I woke up with the smell of rotting bodies in my nose. Other times I dreamt about fighting my way through thick smoke. I saw flashes and heard the noise of shrapnel shattering around me. In a dream one night I saw a row of poppies blooming along the top of a trench and sunlight glinting on bayonets; the colour of the flowers mirrored on steel.

Shortly after I put the bike together, I went bush. The temperature was over a century and the heat was punishing. For three days I rode for a while and walked for a while, always back-tracking to my startin' point. I'd been tormented by the question of whether I'd betrayed Danny by helping Karl, but had shifted the question into deep recesses of my mind. Now, from a distance, the worry of it all gushed like a fountain that'd just been turned on.

I don't know, or remember, how I got home, but I remember wakin' up in hospital with burns to my face, neck and legs. They told me it was the worst case of sunstroke they'd ever seen. As I started to recover I started to cry. It felt like I was standin' outside myself watchin' my heart break to smithereens. The sun of my country had melted me to the bone and I felt the suffering of people like Danny, Patrick and Karl.

The time I'd spent with Patrick in England and the high jinks Danny an' I had got up to in the war and before, got fankled up with each other. Although Danny had never met Patrick, it was like, by some weird process, Danny's features became superimposed under Patrick's black locks makin' my Irish friend whole again.

One day, while still in hospital, the realisation came to me that perhaps the dead can call the living to account for their actions. I knew then that I'd done the right thing by Karl. I understood that Danny would've done the same. I began to feel free of the burden of guilt for having helped my enemy. When I pushed the memories of war behind a veil that I could peel off and revisit if I chose, the weight of remembrance became small, and like a wallet in my hip pocket, easier to carry. The nightmares ceased.

The day I came home from hospital, Mrs Coffey came round. She kept staring at me. Pleading like.

I asked her if she wanted to talk about Danny.

She whispered, 'Yes.'

She accepted my lies about how Danny had died in my arms saying things about home. I described how he single-handedly blew up a nest of German artillery men. We didn't talk about the thousands of Australian boys who never came home, only about Danny.

A few days later, my mother told me she'd bumped into Danny's mother down the main street and she was bringing me a surprise. She'd hardly finished telling me this when I heard a knock on the door and a dog barking.

'I want you to have Bonza,' Mrs Coffey said with sadness in her smile. 'Danny would've liked that.'

I'd forgotten about the dog, but by the way he leapt up on me, he remembered me. He licked and leapt and turned in circles and came back again. He lay on his back and let me scratch his belly. His legs twitched with pleasure.

'Don't know what to say, Mrs Coffey. Are you sure you want to do this?'

'Never been surer, Harry. I just hope he puts some pleasure into your life.'

Bonza and I romped around while the two women had a cup of tea and shortbread. When Mrs Coffey left, the dog and I went for a wander down to the river.

After that, whenever I saw Mrs Coffey, I'd see Danny's grinning face right beside her. Patrick's courage and tenacity, teamed with Danny's outrageous sense of fun, buoyed me up in the dark times.

As time went on, Mrs Coffey's visits got less frequent. Now and again I'd meet her on the street. She'd ask about Bonza, we'd smile at each other then go our separate ways.

<h1 style="text-align:center">25</h1>

Christmas 1919
Langley Berks

Dear Harry

I am sorry to bring you the sad news that Patrick died on Christmas Eve. He asked me before he died to send you these few mementos of the times you shared with him in the war. He was anxious that you should know that your friendship sustained him during your visit here. For Pat, the last few months were filled with pain, doctors and surgery. He was resigned to dying and although I will always miss him, I could never wish him back to the terrible suffering of this last year.

There has been one happy event. Patrick and I got married in June. It was a very quiet affair. There's more – I am due to have his baby in March next year. What a wonderful memorial to Pat that will be. We are all busy knitting and sewing for this new little person whose name will honour my husband.

Patrick told me some things about the dark days of war. He also told me about the time between fighting when he learned the tricks of two-up and about the frog race.

Do you remember last Christmas when you were here and we gathered around the piano? We sang 'Pack up your Troubles' and 'It's a long way to Tipperary' and you recited Banjo Paterson's 'Santa Claus in the Bush'? That was the happiest time for all of us and especially for Pat. He never really picked up after you sailed for home except for a brief period when we exchanged our wedding vows. After that, he became despondent and lost the will to write and eventually, in spite of his happiness about the baby, the will to live. Please know that we are indebted to you.

Perhaps one day in the future, our paths will cross again. I hope that repatriation has been easy for you. It would be wonderful to hear from you but I will understand if letter writing is not one of your strong points. Love to you and to yours from a grateful friend.

Caitlin O'Hare

***

I took my time opening the package. I tried not to think too much about the last time I'd seen Patrick. Images of him out of breath, struggling with eating, drinking and speaking were vivid. Inside the package was a full-face balaclava with a note in Patrick's handwriting saying,

I know you'll say, what do I want with a bloody balaclava in an Australian summer? It's to remind you of the night of The Great Race of the Frogs, when we got drunk, ate apples and sung ourselves hoarse. The night we stumbled over the dying German – the night we buried him. Remember?

The tobacco tin was tucked inside. It also had a note stuck to it.

Hey, Harry! Remember we fought over this? Well, you can have it now. I traced Karl Grottenthaler's mother and mailed the letters, photos and rosary I took from Karl that night in the war. For some reason, I couldn't part with the tin. The decision is yours now. Her address is

Frau Grottenthaler,
Bergenstrasse 42,
Garmisch,
Germany 3926.

The edges of the tin were smooth. I imagined that Patrick had kept it in a pocket, so that friction between fabric and metal had rounded the corners. Karl's leave passes were still inside. I touched them, closed the lid and held the tin close to my chest. It felt warm, the way a friendship sometimes does when the conditions that shaped the bond lie back in the past.

What we call the beginning is often the end
And to make an end is to make a beginning.
The end is where we start from…

T.S. Eliot, 'Little Gidding '

Acknowledgements

Thank you

always and ever to Keith, who read many drafts of this work; I cherish his wise, witty ways that still glow like a lambent light to warm me with memories;

to Paul, Anne Marie, Leigh, Dale, Courtney and Mackenzie for teaching me the true value of life;

to Bryce for his advice on military standards and war events and clever artwork;

to Norm Hutchinson: I am privileged and honoured to have had access to his father's war diaries and memorabilia;

to Professor Tom Shapcott, who planted the seed for this story and for his generous advice and encouragement during my Honours year at Adelaide University;

to my friends in the W.I.P. group – Steph, Amy, Chelsea and Henry – for their collective and ongoing encouragement;

to a wide, wide network of family and friends too numerous to mention, for taking the time to listen to the woes of an emerging writer.